The
FLiP
FLOP
Club

Star Struck

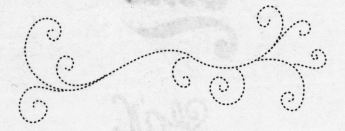

Ellen Richardson

Series created by Working Partners Ltd

OXFORD
UNIVERSITY PRESS

OXFORD
UNIVERSITY PRESS

Great Clarendon Street, Oxford OX2 6DP

Oxford University Press is a department of the University of Oxford.
It furthers the University's objective of excellence in research, scholarship,
and education by publishing worldwide in

Oxford   New York

Auckland   Cape Town   Dar es Salaam   Hong Kong   Karachi
Kuala Lumpur   Madrid   Melbourne   Mexico City   Nairobi
New Delhi   Shanghai   Taipei   Toronto

With offices in

Argentina   Austria   Brazil   Chile   Czech Republic   France   Greece
Guatemala   Hungary   Italy   Japan   Poland   Portugal   Singapore
South Korea   Switzerland   Thailand   Turkey   Ukraine   Vietnam

Oxford is a registered trade mark of Oxford University Press
in the UK and in certain other countries

British Library Cataloguing in Publication Data
Data available

ISBN: 978-0-19-275664-0
1 3 5 7 9 10 8 6 4 2

Printed in Great Britain

Paper used in the production of this book is a natural,
recyclable product made from wood grown in sustainable forests.
The manufacturing process conforms to the environmental
regulations of the country of origin.

For Rozzy and Gillian

SUNDAY ISLAND

N
W · E
S

DEAD MAN'S

THE HOOK

ROCKY CLIFFS

MIRROR COVE

Treeb

WESTERN ISLES

DEVIL'S TEETH

MOUNTAIN STREAM

LAKE

Caravan Park

MAIN BEACH

HARBOUR

H

Sailing Club

EASTERN
ISLES

DY
WS

Stables

Sunday
House

SOMMER
-ON-
SEA

RING ROAD

CAUSEWAY

urch
aveyard

Village

Aunt
Dina's
Cottage

Chapter 1

'One more time, guys!' Sierra jabbed at her iPod.

Elly groaned as the *thud, thud, thud* of the electronic bass and drums started up again. Much as she loved The Sparks' hit single, 'All Together Now', she'd had enough. Her throat was sore from singing and her legs ached from dancing.

'Oh no you don't.' Tash staggered across the room and collapsed face down on her bed. 'You've promised "one more time" for hours now.'

'I need a break too.' Elly sank onto the

floor of Tash's bedroom. They'd cleared a big space in the middle to make a dance studio. 'My legs and brain have stopped talking to each other.'

'Come on, guys!' Sierra flicked her long dark hair over her shoulder. 'You're not trying. The singing's good but, Tash, you've got to get the dance steps sorted or we'll never win *Tomorrow's Stars!*'

Tash groaned loudly. She rolled over to look at Sierra. 'It's easy for you. Dancing's your thing. I can't help it if I'm good at surfing and sailing but rubbish at dancing.'

'Tash, you're not rubbish, just tired,' Elly 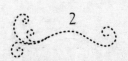 cut in, seeing Sierra's face grow stubborn. She knew how much their friend wanted to win the talent contest and appear on stage at Sunday Island's music festival. But she and Tash needed a break. 'We've been practising all day, Sierra.' Elly bit back a smile as a sneaky  but brilliant idea flitted into her head. 'I don't know about you, but I'm hungry.'

Sierra sniffed. 'You're not gonna get me with that one. I know I'm a greedy pig, but there are more important things than food. Well, sometimes.'

'OK.' Elly shrugged. 'I'll just have to take Aunt Dina's special spicy gingerbread cookies back home with me and tell her you didn't like them.'

Sierra's eyes grew wide. 'Gingerbread? The ones that are sort of chewy, but melt in your mouth?' Her stubborn frown faded into a dreamy look as Elly nodded. 'Where are they?'

'In my backpack.' Elly stopped trying to hide her grin.

'Training does burn up loads of calories,'

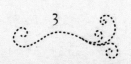

Sierra announced. 'I'll fetch the lemonade, you get the cookies.' Sierra picked up the jug of lemonade, home-made by Tash's butler, Jasper, and plonked it on the floor near Elly. 'We can talk costumes, hair, and make-up while we eat. I've brought research material,' she said. She held her giant purple handbag upside down and dumped its contents. Out showered lip gloss, hair wax, sparkly headbands and hair clips, nail varnish in bright glittery red, purple, and pink, and half a dozen glossy magazines.

Elly lifted the plastic tub full of homemade cookies out of her backpack. She prised off the lid and a rich, warm smell of cinnamon and ginger drifted through the room. Tash groaned once more, but this time it was a happy sound. She shoved herself off the bed

and padded across
the floor to sit cross-
legged beside them. 'I
might live after all.'

Elly's stomach gave a demanding growl, then relented as she bit into a cookie. She rinsed it down with a swallow of lemonade. Delicious!

Sierra demolished three cookies, then grabbed a copy of *Music Trend* and opened to a two-page spread. ***This Year's Hottest New Girl Band!*** shrieked the headline.

'The Sparks!' Elly swallowed a mouthful of cookie and bent forward to get a better look. 'Wow,' she sighed. 'Don't they look totally amazing? Why can't I ever look like that?' The three members of the girl band wore sparkly jackets over their jeans and T-shirts. The jackets were embroidered to look like exploding fireworks. Marina, the guitarist, glinted in green and gold; Abi, on keyboard, sparkled silvery blue; and Lou, the drummer, dazzled in hot pink.

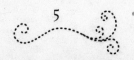

Sierra snorted. 'Because you haven't got a personal make-up artist and stylist. But you're right. They look great. Lou is just so cool.' Sierra pointed to the image of the tall, slender girl who sat perched at her drum kit, smiling at the camera, her long hair dyed a vivid red. 'I read that she started the drums at five and got her first gig as a drummer touring with a rock band at sixteen.'

'She's good.' Tash nodded. 'But Abi is super-talented. Keyboard holds everything together, and she does all the electronic stuff, like the bass. Plus she's a great singer. Did you know she cycled across China last year on a charity ride for Disaster Aid? How cool is that?'

'I read about that too,' said Elly. The photo of Abi showed a petite, smiling young woman standing behind her keyboard, with her

short black hair and large dark eyes ringed with eyeliner and massive fake lashes. 'And she is really pretty. But I like Marina best.'

Elly's eyes returned to the guitarist. She wasn't as dramatic-looking as the other two band members. She was average height and had softly curling brown hair and freckles. In fact, Elly thought, she looked so nice-but-ordinary that you would hardly notice her if you saw her on the street, unless you looked into her eyes. There was something in them that grabbed your attention. 'She writes all their songs; not just the words, but the music too. And when she sings, you can see that she really means it. She's not just performing.'

'Marina is a genius,' Sierra agreed. 'But she really ought to do something with her hair. I mean, if she wasn't wearing about twenty glamour rings, a nose piercing, and those gorgeous shoes she'd look just like my RE teacher at school.'

'My RE teacher has double nose piercings *and* five tattoos,' Elly said. 'Your school needs to work on its image.'

Tash snorted, then started in surprise as the door burst open and Mojo raced into the room. The border terrier was whimpering, his tail tucked between his legs. He made a beeline for Tash and jumped into her lap with a whine.

She cuddled him in her arms. 'What is it, Mojo?' The dog whimpered more loudly. Tash lifted her head to look at Elly and Sierra. 'Something's really scared him.'

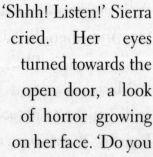

'Shhh! Listen!' Sierra cried. Her eyes turned towards the open door, a look of horror growing on her face. 'Do you hear that?'

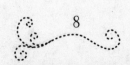

Elly heard it now: a strange wailing cry drifted upstairs and through the door. It wavered, died, then rose to an unholy shriek.

'Oh my godfathers!' Sierra yelped, jumping to her feet. 'What is that?'

'Whatever it is, it's scared Mojo half to death. You stay here, Mojo.' Tash placed the dog on her bed. He whined and cowered. 'I know,' Tash said. 'It's a nasty noise, but you'll be safe here.' She whirled round to face her friends. 'I'm going to investigate. That could be an animal caught in a trap or something. I've never heard anything like it in my life.'

'I'm coming with you!' Elly shoved the lid on the remaining cookies and leapt up. The strange cry had dwindled away, but now it began again. 'The poor thing needs help. Besides, I've just got to find out what sort of animal makes that weird sound.'

'But it could be dangerous. Let's consider our options,' Sierra wailed, as Tash and Elly grabbed her by the hands and pulled her out of the door after them.

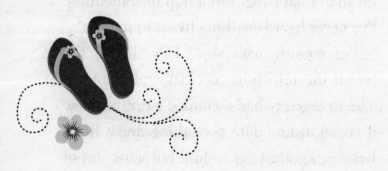

Chapter 2

Elly ran downstairs after Tash. Sierra followed more slowly.

'Aaaarrrrreeeeeeeee . . . Owwwww . . .' The noise seemed to come from all directions at once. Tash scrambled down the staircase and slid to a stop beside the door to her mum's office. 'Mum?' Tash pushed the door open and stuck her head inside.

'That's weird,' Tash said. 'She's not there. I thought she was working today.' Tash cocked her head, listening to the wail dwindle then grow. 'I'm not sure the noise is coming from the house at all. Let's check outside.'

Tash raced towards the front door. Elly followed, scurrying past gloomy paintings and faded wallpaper, and caught up with Tash at the front door. Her friend had come to a sudden stop, her hand on the doorknob. Elly felt the back of her neck prickle with goosebumps as the mysterious sound grew louder, more insistent, almost like someone chanting. 'Ugh . . . ugh . . . ugh . . . ugh.'

'Is it in pain or just angry?' Sierra panted as she caught up with them. 'Only it sounds like it's bigger than us and guess what? I forgot to go to my animal self-defence class last week.' She shot them a weak grin.

'Come on.' Tash hooked her arm through 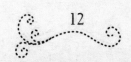Sierra's. 'You've got all the dance moves. You can always kick your way out of any trouble.'

'You're just skiving off rehearsal,' Sierra said as Tash opened the front door.

'That horrible noise
is coming from the
garage!' Tash shouted.
She jumped off the front steps
and disappeared around the side of the house.

'Why does she always do this?' Sierra
moaned as she and Elly sprinted to catch up
with their friend.

Elly didn't have the breath to answer. Tash
had disappeared inside the garage. Elly and
Sierra followed her into the dim interior. It
was empty inside: only oil-stained concrete
and . . . noise! 'Aaaaah . . . ohhhh . . . ' It was
coming from overhead. Elly found herself
staring at the ceiling.

'It's in the games room!' Tash cried and
raced for a staircase that led to the garage's
long, narrow attic.

'But how did it get up there?' Sierra
protested as Elly pushed past her up the stairs
after Tash. 'I mean, if it's so wounded?'

Tash didn't answer. She paused at the closed door at the top of the stairs, took one nervous look back at Elly, turned the handle and stepped through.

The noise flooded Elly's ears, plinky and strummy now, as well as whiny. She followed Tash into the games room and slid to a stop, unable to believe the sight that met her eyes.

The next second Sierra crashed into her from behind, nearly knocking them both to the floor. 'Oh sorry! I . . . I . . . ' Sierra's voice trailed off. 'I don't believe it!' she wailed. 'Oh Dad, this is so embarrassing.'

'Mum!' cried Tash.

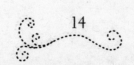

Elly found her voice had dried up completely. Aunt Dina stood in the middle of the garage's narrow attic room. Light from windows in the slanting roof shone down like stage spotlights. Aunt Dina was dressed in a retro-seventies maxi dress, her long black hair dripping with beads. She was swaying and crooning and snapping her fingers. Sierra's father, Mr Cruz, stood on one side of her, strumming an old-fashioned-looking guitar. On the other side, banging on a tambourine, twisting and twirling and stamping her feet, was Tash's mum. Elly could hardly believe it was Mrs Blake-Reynolds underneath the tie-die smock, ripped jeans, and platform boots, except that Tash was bent double with a huge case of the giggles.

The three grown-up voices stuttered to a stop. Elly winced as Aunt Dina's last note went flat. Her aunt had a gorgeous speaking voice, but unfortunately she was tone deaf. Standing next to her in church during the hymns was agony, especially as Aunt Dina loved singing, and singing *loudly*.

'Well,' Tash said. 'At least we know no animal has been injured in the making of this music video. Except Mojo. He's hiding on my bed, Mum. You guys scared him half to death.'

'Perhaps the dog has not got an ear for music, hmm?' Mr Cruz's fingers sped over the guitar, deftly plucking the strings. A lilting Spanish melody filled the garage. He beamed at them. He's really good, Elly thought. The guitar sounds great, as long as Aunt Dina isn't singing!

'What are you doing?' Sierra interrupted. 'Hiding away in here and scaring dogs and children?'

'That shouldn't take much guesswork, as it isn't rocket science, nuclear physics or even quadratic equations.' Aunt Dina smiled at them. 'We're practising for the contest tomorrow.'

Elly's mouth fell open. It must be a mistake.
Surely her aunt wasn't going to make that
noise *in public*. Surely she wasn't going to
stand on a stage in front of strangers and all
her friends on the island looking like that?
'You . . . you don't mean *Tomorrow's Stars?*'

Aunt Dina grinned at her. 'Don't you
approve?'

'Well, I . . . I . . . ' Elly trailed off. She
couldn't possibly tell Aunt Dina that her
singing sounded like a cat drowning in a vat
of tomato ketchup. Or that she was way too
old to go around with beads in her hair. 'No.
That's just . . . great. I'm so pleased. And . . .
surprised.'

Her aunt frowned in confusion. 'Because
we're entering too,' Elly added quickly.

'So we meet our competition! Some of it,
at least.' Mrs Blake-Reynolds's bright blue

eyes twinkled at them from beneath her tie-dyed bandana. 'Well then, you've seen our performance, what about showing us yours?'

'No. That's not a good ide—' Tash began.

'Why not?' Sierra interrupted. 'Practising in front of an audience should help.'

'No! It's not ready yet.' Tash's face had gone bright red.

'Hey, but—'

'No, Sierra!' Tash snapped.

She's nervous! Elly realized. Tash was actually trembling. 'Yeah,' Elly said quickly, 'you guys are going to have to wait until the talent show tomorrow. I want our performance to be a surprise.'

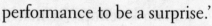

'I can't wait!' Aunt Dina beamed at them. 'Will you at least tell us what you're singing? We're doing a "Scarborough Fair" medley.'

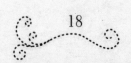

'Scarborough what? . . . I mean, yeah, that was really excellent.' Sierra's face was nearly as red as Tash's. 'And I love the clothes. Although, Dad, I'd think about ditching the waistcoat. It's sort of . . . orange.'

Mr Cruz nodded and patted his velvet waistcoat. 'Very seventies,' he said with a satisfied smile. 'We searched many charity shops to find these clothes.'

'You girls better get on with your own rehearsal and leave us to practise,' Aunt Dina said. 'Otherwise you'll have no excuse when we win tomorrow.'

'Absolutely,' Sierra said, with her brightest smile.

'Oh, and can I ask a favour?' Aunt Dina strode to the back of the room, her maxi dress rustling, the beads in her hair gently clinking, and returned carrying a large plastic food box. 'I made far too many cookies. Would you mind popping into town later and delivering these to my friend Dorothy? I was going to do it myself, but the others seem to think we need a bit more practice.' She held the plastic container out to Elly. 'I thought we sounded pretty good.'

'Uh . . . yeah, really original, Aunt Dina.' Elly grabbed the box of cookies, a wide smile frozen on her face. Elly didn't want to hurt her aunt's feelings, but 'pretty good' were not the words she'd use to describe the noise the adults had been making. 'Great. Um, gotta go!' She turned and fled. Sierra was already halfway out of the door, Tash hard on her heels.

'Let's head into town straight away,' Elly suggested, when she'd caught them up outside the garage. 'They'll be setting up the festival now: all the tents and stages. I want to go and look.'

'Great idea,' Tash said quickly.

Sierra's eyes brightened. 'Maybe we'll spot some of the acts!'

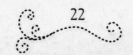

Chapter 3

The town was like a crowded beehive: tourists swarmed and bumbled up every street. Hot, sweaty bodies trickled along in queues. Sierra dodged after Tash, her purple handbag dangling from her shoulder. Elly grabbed the handbag's strap and held tight: if they got separated it would take ages to find each other again. Tash carried Mojo to keep him from being trampled underfoot. The girls threaded their way through the crowd single-file.

'Wow! I've never seen it this busy,' Tash shouted over her shoulder. Mojo woofed in agreement; he seemed happy to have left the strange noises of Sunday House behind.

'The Sunday Island Music Festival is getting popular,' Sierra said. 'Especially this year with the *Tomorrow's Stars* contest and a chance to perform on the main stage.'

'There's supposed to be some surprise announcement. They were able to get a really famous group at the last minute—oof!' A man bumped into Elly, nearly knocking the cookies from under her arm.

'Careful!' Sierra ordered. 'I'm hoping we'll get a few of those.'

'You ate tons at the house,' Elly said, tucking the box back under her arm and grabbing hold of Sierra's bag again. 'You can't be hungry.'

'Of course I can! Hey, look at those guys over there.' Sierra pointed to a quartet of young men wearing expensively scruffy jeans,

designer stubble,
and watches the
size of goose eggs
strapped to their wrists.
'I bet that's one of the acts. Do you
recognize them?'

'No . . . but they certainly look like a boy
band.' Elly pulled her festival brochure out
of her back pocket. It was falling apart from
being folded and refolded so many times. She
scanned the list of acts. 'The Alpha Boys are
playing, and Chasin' Fame.'

'And Dazzle!' Sierra cried, peering over
Elly's shoulder at the leaflet. 'Hey, maybe
those guys were Dazzle!'

'Pete will be thrilled you thought he was a
pop star,' Tash said with a grin. 'Those guys
work at the sailing club.'

Sierra shrugged and adjusted her sunglasses
on her nose. 'Sailors aren't supposed to wear
so much bling. Unless they're pirates!'

'I'll tell him you said that.' Tash laughed.

Elly refolded her brochure with a sigh and stuck it back in her pocket. 'I'm dying to know which famous group is coming to the festival. When are they going to announce it?'

'The festival organizers have kept that totally secret.' Tash shrugged. 'My own mum won't tell me. It's someone big though.'

'It's so cool your mum is one of the festival organizers,' Elly said. 'She'll get to meet all the stars.'

'I know!' Tash grinned. 'Pop music isn't exactly her thing, but she's so good at the organizing part. She's been on the phone all the time, raising money and sorting everything out. And she's actually been playing decent music on her iPod for once. She's downloaded all the acts.'

'Hey!' Elly gasped. 'What if—'

'No mystery act on her

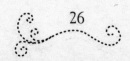

26

iPod.' Tash shrugged.
'I already checked.
Sorry.'

'Let's get out
of here. I'm getting
claustrophobic.' Sierra gave Tash a gentle
shove. 'I want to get to Melody Meadows and
look for pop stars.'

'After we deliver the cookies,' Elly said.
They were near the edge of the town and the
crowd was starting to thin out.

'Who's getting the cookies again?' Sierra
asked. 'Do you want me to carry them?'

'Eat them, you mean.' Elly hugged the
plastic box close. 'No way.'

'I would not. Well, maybe one . . . '

'Nope. These are for Dorothy,' Elly said.
'She's pretty old and lives on her own. I think
she came along to one of Aunt Dina's painting
classes and they got to be friends. Dorothy's
always in her garden or out walking with her
binoculars. She's a twitcher.'

'Oh,' Sierra cried. 'Is that a disease? Poor thing.'

'It means bird watcher, bird brain,' Tash cut in. 'You don't know much about nature, do you?'

'Maybe not.' Sierra tossed her hair over her shoulder. 'But I am a genius on clothes, computers, swimming, dancing, and music. *And* I'm our best chance of winning *Tomorrow's Stars*. So let's get these cookies delivered and get back to work.'

Tash groaned.

Elly turned down Sunnyfield Lane and the others followed. Tash put Mojo down now they had left the crowds behind, and the border terrier trotted ahead of them, pausing to sniff at clumps of weeds or muddy stones. Small houses lined the street, front

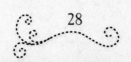

gardens with careful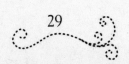
displays of driftwood,
large seashells, or
skeletons of starfish and
sponges on the garden walls.

At the very end of the winding street sat a small stone cottage covered in climbing roses. The front garden was crammed with lavender and rosemary, white rock roses and pink thrift. The scent of lavender and roses filled the air in the warm sunshine. A sleek young tabby cat, its front and paws gleaming white, sat curled on the step.

'Woof!' Mojo raced towards the cat, which sprang to its feet with a hiss.

'Mojo, no!' Elly cried.

'It's OK,' Tash said. 'He loves cats.'

'But do they love him?' Sierra asked. The cat jabbed a paw at the border terrier. Mojo leapt back, then rolled onto his back and stuck his feet up in the air. He whined encouragingly at the cat, which watched him for a moment, then turned a haughty shoulder and began to groom its paws. Mojo sat up and cocked his head at the girls, as though to say: What do I do now?

'See?' Tash said with a laugh. 'Practically best friends already. Stay here, Mojo.'

Elly led the way to the door and Sierra pressed the doorbell. 'Bye bye, cookies,' Sierra said sadly.

Tash's snort was interrupted as the door swung open to reveal a slender woman with short white hair and a tanned face. Her hazel eyes lit up when she saw them and she gave them a warm smile.

'Elly! Lovely to meet you again. Has Dina sent you? Do come in.'

'Aunt Dina's been baking again,' Elly said, as they followed Dorothy into the tiny, stone-floored

hall. 'She thought you might like some cookies.'

'They're scrummy!' Sierra chimed in.

Dorothy laughed. 'Well, in that case, you'd better join me for a cup of tea and some cookies. If you'd like that?'

'I'd love it!' Sierra said. 'I'm Sierra and that's Tash.'

'I thought we were rehearsing,' Elly reminded her.

'Oh, are you entering *Tomorrow's Stars?*' Dorothy asked. 'I don't want to hold you up, but I'd love to hear about your plans.'

'Good,' Tash said. 'I'm rubbish at dancing, so I'd much rather have a cup of tea.'

'I'm sure you're not rubbish,' Dorothy said, as she showed them into the sitting room. 'Make yourselves comfortable while I get the tea.'

'Can I help you?' Sierra asked.

'That would be lovely. But only one of you,'

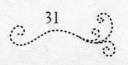

Dorothy said as Elly stepped forward too. 'My kitchen is tiny.'

Sierra followed Dorothy out of the room. Elly spotted a group of framed photos on the mantel over the fireplace and wandered over to have a look.

'This must be a group of Dorothy's students at a concert,' Elly said to Tash. 'She's a music teacher. This photo looks like it was taken a long time ago; her hair's quite dark.' A younger Dorothy smiled out of the photograph, surrounded by a group of happy young people holding guitars, flutes, and violins.

'I wonder who that is.' Tash pointed to another old, slightly faded photograph of a young girl aged about ten or eleven, holding hands with a beaming dark-haired Dorothy.

'She looks nice.' For some reason the girl

looked familiar, but that didn't make sense. The photo was probably taken before Elly was even born.

'That's my granddaughter, Em, when she was about your age.' Dorothy bustled into the room, carrying a laden tray. Sierra followed with a teapot. 'She's coming for the festival and I can't wait to see her. Work keeps her far too busy these days. Choose a perch, girls, and we'll sample Dina's baking. If I know your aunt, Elly, I bet these cookies taste even better than they smell.'

Sierra sat next to Dorothy on the sofa and scoffed half a dozen cookies, beaming at their hostess. 'Dancing makes you hungry, but these are the perfect solution. Yum!'

'You've been working hard. I always used to tell my students: success is one per cent inspiration and ninety-nine per cent perspiration. In other words, dreams aren't enough—you've got to work at what you love. So, I think it's time you sang for your supper. How about a show?'

Tash choked on a crumb. 'I-I don't think that's a good idea. We're not ready . . .' Her voice stumbled to a stop.

'Everyone has stage fright, Tash,' Dorothy said gently.

'I'm just no good! Sierra's a fab dancer and Elly's going to be an actor like her mum. I'm letting them down.' Tash's cheeks were scarlet. She looked close to tears, and Elly bit her lip. Poor Tash!

'You're not!' Elly cried. 'You've got a great singing voice.'

'What she said,' Sierra added. 'And you can do the dance steps if you try. Come on, Tash. You never give up.'

'Maybe I can help.

I'll tell you a secret.' Dorothy sat up straight in her chair, her eyes on Tash. 'I used to perform in the West End.'

'What?' Elly stared at their hostess. She couldn't believe it—a West End actress!

'Only in the chorus.' Dorothy laughed. 'And only for a few years. But I learnt a lot, those few years as a chorus girl. I still know how to put a number over to the audience, and I'm happy to give you some pointers. But you will have to sing and dance for me, Tash. Are you brave enough? I'm not *that* scary, am I?' Her eyes twinkled with laughter, and Elly thought again how nice Aunt Dina's friend was.

'Well *I'm* terrified now!' Sierra gave a mock shiver. 'But I'm game if you guys are.' She looked at Elly and Tash, practically bouncing with excitement and impatience.

Sierra might be keen, but Tash looked ready

to run for it, Elly thought. She gave her friend a reassuring smile.

Tash took a deep breath. 'OK,' she said. 'After all, I'm going to have to perform for real tomorrow.' She put the remains of her cookie down on her plate, looking slightly sick.

Elly jumped to her feet and grabbed Tash's hand before she could change her mind. Sierra joined them as they cleared a space in the middle of the sitting room and turned to face Dorothy, who sat on the edge of the sofa, eyes sparkling with excitement.

'We'll have to sing without the backing track,' Elly said. 'Tash, you start us off—you've got the best ear.'

Tash gave a squeak of dismay, then threw her head back, squared her shoulders and opened her mouth: *'We're back together… all together now. Bad*

times are over . . . we'll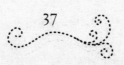
rise above the storm.'

Elly joined in, singing,
smiling, dancing: it was
hard, but she loved it, and soon
forgot she was performing for an audience of
one. She could feel Tash and Sierra giving
it their all, especially when they reached the
chorus: *All together now and for ever!*

Her heart was thudding with excitement
and pride. At last the song came to an end,
and they'd done it better than ever before.
The Sparks would have been proud of them!

'Well done!' Dorothy jumped to her feet
and gave them a group hug. 'And a brilliant
choice of song, if you don't mind my saying
so. You performed it like pros. I would say
you girls stand a very good chance of winning
tomorrow. But there is just one thing that I
think might help with the dance steps. Watch
me on the sideways slide and kick.'

Elly watched as the elderly woman seemed

to shed twenty years and glide into the steps they'd been practising all morning. Except that Dorothy did them perfectly. First time. Wow, she really was a pro! Elly thought as she stared, amazed.

'Do you see?' Dorothy turned to them. 'Hop on the left foot twice and then go into the slide. It'll sort your problem with the timing, Tash. Try it.'

Tash glided around the room, doing one hop, slide, and kick after another, slowly at first, then faster and faster. 'Hey! It works! Look, Sierra, I can do it now!' Tash's smile looked three metres wide. 'Thank you, Dorothy!'

'Yes,' said Elly. 'Thanks so much!'

'My hero!' Sierra said, giving Dorothy a kiss on the cheek. 'Will you give me dance lessons this summer? Please?'

'You hardly need them, my dear. Whoever's been teaching you has done a good job. I wouldn't want to interfere. 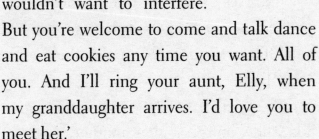 But you're welcome to come and talk dance and eat cookies any time you want. All of you. And I'll ring your aunt, Elly, when my granddaughter arrives. I'd love you to meet her.'

Elly couldn't stop smiling as she, Tash, and Sierra said goodbye and left. Tash was much happier, which was great. And Dorothy had said they were good enough to win *Tomorrow's Stars*. They had a chance. A real chance!

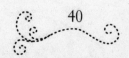

Chapter 4

Tash strode ahead of them down the path, throwing sticks for Mojo to chase, looking relaxed for the first time that day.

'Well, Tash is happier.' Sierra grinned at Elly. 'Dorothy is so cool. I'm going to try and get a dance lesson out of her somehow. She's totally fabulous.'

As Elly opened her mouth to agree, Tash gave a shout of surprise. 'Come and see this, guys!' She was pointing out to sea. Elly squinted and saw a huge yacht rounding the island—a triple-master with all sails set and curved full of wind, heading west at speed

towards the curved spit of land the islanders called the Hook.

'That's fancy,' Sierra said, staring at the yacht with her hands on her hips. 'Rich people coming for the festival, I bet.'

'But why are they headed towards the Hook and not the quay?' Tash wondered. 'Any ship making land on Sunday Island is supposed to report to the Harbour Master with a passenger and cargo list.'

'Ohh!' Sierra squealed. 'I bet they're smugglers! Or pirates.'

Elly's heart skipped a beat. She didn't really believe the yacht was full of pirates, 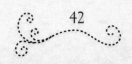 but this mystery needed investigating. 'Let's go to Mirror Cove and see if it anchors there. Maybe it's just sightseers.'

'I refuse to let my pirates and smugglers

turn into boring old tourists!' Sierra cried.

Tash nodded in agreement, eyes sparkling. 'Come on, Mojo!'

Elly and her friends sprinted towards the hillside path leading towards Mirror Cove. It was a long, uphill run over what the islanders fondly called 'The Mountain'. Elly raced up the peaty path, leaping over grey granite boulders and dodging prickly branches of gorse and tangling brambles. She was soon in the lead, leaving even Mojo behind. He scampered after her, barking frantically with excitement.

As she reached the grove of beech trees on the hillside, a flock of quail rose, startled, into the air. 'Sorry!' Elly cried to the birds, and ran on. She felt as if she could run for ever over the peat soil of Sunday Island, under the warm blue sky, with the sea breeze cooling her face. But almost as soon as she finished the thought, she reached the hilltop overlooking Mirror Cove.

And there it was: the yacht. Lying at anchor in the sheltered, secret bay.

'Get down!' Sierra grabbed Elly by the shoulders and tugged her down to crouching. 'You'd never make a spy,' Sierra scolded, as Tash came gasping up, shushing Mojo. The border terrier obediently stopped his excited yaps and panted happily at his mistress.

Tash knelt beside them, holding Mojo with one arm. 'They're launching a motor boat: look! Someone's coming ashore. This is totally not normal! I wonder if we should report them to the Harbour Master.'

Elly watched, heart pounding with excitement, as a man leapt from the deck of the yacht into the small

motor launch towed astern. He tugged the outboard motor into life, cast off the line, then steered the launch around to the side of the yacht nearest shore.

'Look!' hissed Sierra. 'Those are definitely smugglers getting on the launch now. Do they look shady or what?'

Elly nodded, speechless. Three figures scrambled from the yacht into the motor launch, one after another. They wore sunglasses and hoodies pulled up to hide their faces.

'I wish I had my binoculars,' Tash muttered. She leant forward, peering at the launch as it backed away from the yacht, turned in a swirl of spray and headed for the beach.

'Watch out!' Elly yanked Tash back into the shelter of a clump of bracken. 'Look!' she whispered, pointing down to the beach of Mirror Cove. Two figures stepped forward from where they had been hidden at the base of the cliff.

'Meet and greet,' muttered Sierra. 'How the heck did she get down the cliff in *those*?'

Elly looked. One of the people waiting on the beach was a man in a dark suit and tie. Standing next to him was a woman in a jacket, skirt, and very high heels. The sight was so strange she bit her lip to keep from bursting into giggles.

'Weirder and weirder,' Tash said. 'A secret rendezvous at the most secluded cove on Sunday Island. What is going on?'

'Smugglers, pirates . . . or gangsters!' Sierra bounced on her knees, unable to contain her excitement. 'The Suits look just like gangsters. They're wearing sunglasses too. They're all wearing sunglasses! That proves they're up to something!'

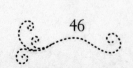

'So are you part of the plot?' Tash asked, tapping Sierra's sunglasses.

'That's fashion! It's totally different . . . ' Sierra's voice faded as Tash snorted with smothered laughter.

'OK, maybe sunglasses don't prove anything. But . . . '

'This is like something out of a film,' Elly agreed.

The launch roared up close to the beach, nearly grounding itself. The three people in hoodies jumped over the side into the shallow water and waded ashore. The suited woman and man rushed down to greet the newcomers, shaking hands eagerly and ushering them up the beach.

'What now?' Tash whispered. 'Are they just going to talk about secret stuff then go back to their yacht, or are they staying on the island? And how did those people in suits get down there?'

'A helicopter?' Elly suggested. 'You can't climb the cliff path in heels. Or . . . oh . . . that's how.' It was hard not to feel a bit cheated. The suited woman was teetering on one foot, slipping her shoes off and depositing them in a glossy handbag before tugging on trainers. The hoodies had waded ashore barefoot. Now they sat down on the sand, pulling on the shoes they had been carrying.

'They're going to climb up,' Tash hissed. 'We've got to hide!' She began to back up on hands and knees, taking Mojo with her. Elly and Sierra followed. Once they were far enough away from the cliff top, they stood up. Elly scanned the hillside, looking for cover.

'Over there,' she whispered, pointing to a trio of scrubby pine trees further down the hill away from the path to town. 'We can watch from there.'

'Spies Are Us!' Sierra said with a nervous giggle and darted for shelter. Elly followed. Tash took off the long scarf she wore threaded through the loops of her shorts for a belt and attached it to Mojo's collar. She trotted after Elly and Sierra, tugging the reluctant dog after her.

'Be good, Mojo!' Tash whispered sternly to the border terrier, as she joined them behind the trees. 'He knows people are coming up the cliff and wants to make friends,' she said.

'Spies don't have friends, Mojo,' Sierra explained with mock sadness. Then she shivered with delight and nerves. 'Oohh! This is exciting, but a bit scary. What if they spot us watching them? We might be swimming with the fishes or wearing concrete overshoes or—'

'I didn't notice them carrying any bags

of concrete,' Tash said drily. 'Do you mean snorkelling?'

'Haven't you ever seen an old gangster film?' Elly said with an exasperated sigh. 'My mum was an extra in one once. That's what gangsters do to their enemies. It's not a good thing.'

'Shhhh!' Sierra pointed.

A head popped over the cliff edge. It wore a dark grey hoodie. The owner pulled themself upright and reached down to help a second person up. Another hoodie. The third followed. Then two of the people in hoodies reached down and helped the woman in the suit clamber to the top of the cliff.

'Oh, my nails are shattered!' A distressed voice, and a splutter of sympathetic laughter from the hoodies, drifted on the wind to Elly. Then the man climbed up and all five people walked quickly and purposefully away on the path towards town.

'What do we do now?' Sierra asked. 'This is no way for a mystery to end!'

'Well, I suppose we could follow—' Elly broke off. Sierra's phone had sounded. The familiar noise echoed across the cliff top. Thank goodness that hadn't happened two minutes ago, she thought, as Sierra fished her bright pink phone out of her handbag and jabbed at it.

'Hello? Oh, hi, Dad. What's up?' Sierra fell silent. Elly watched as her eyes grew round with excitement. 'Wow. OK, thanks for tipping me off.' Sierra hung up and grinned at them. 'News. Mega news. The word in town is that the famous surprise act for the festival is coming to the island today! Forget smugglers and gangsters, we need to get back to town and look out for them. I'm dying to know who they are.'

'But . . . what about your gangsters?' Tash cried. 'They're getting away!'

'Spies, you mean,' Sierra corrected. 'And pop stars are more exciting.'

Elly stared from Sierra to Tash and back again. They hadn't got it. '*Hello?* Wake up, you two! We've just witnessed the mystery band being smuggled onto Sunday Island: that's who the hoodies are!'

Tash stared at her blankly. Then she exploded: 'Of course! You are so smart!' Mojo yelped in surprise and gazed up at his mistress with a hurt expression.

'Clever old Elly.' Sierra grinned and gave Elly a hug. 'Gosh, they must be really famous to go to all that trouble not to be spotted. Let's go and investigate. One mystery solved, one to go!'

Chapter 5

'They'll be heading for Melody Meadows,' Tash said. 'I'd bet on that. I know a shortcut. We can cut round and see if I'm right.' She untied her scarf from Mojo's collar and, with a grin at Elly and Sierra, began jogging down the hill to the path the mysterious trio had taken a few minutes before.

Sierra shrugged. 'Well, it's a plan, I guess.' She trotted after Tash and Elly fell in step beside her. Soon they were loping along the path through the beech grove. The dim light filtering through the crinkled oval leaves was cool and pleasant after the hot sunshine on

the headland. Elly knew she was right: the secretive, hooded visitors to Sunday Island had to be the mystery band. But which band?

Suddenly, Tash veered off the path, ducking under a low branch and down a rutted track Elly hadn't spotted before. They dodged fallen branches and tree roots. And then, just as suddenly, the trees stopped and Elly found herself scampering down a steep hillside spotted with gorse and bracken. Melody Meadows lay below them: a large, irregular oval of grass and wild flowers where the island's one herd of Jersey cows often grazed.

But not now. Elly gasped. The normally peaceful meadow was transformed.

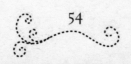

It was ringed with a high board fence. Barricades were being erected at the gates. Banners and flags fluttered in the strong sea breeze, and much of the meadow was covered in tents and stands. The main stage stood at one end, tall and commanding, with giant video screens either side and enormous loudspeakers crowded round. The crackle of a sound system being tested filled the air. Dozens of busy, harassed-looking people, most dressed in shorts and T-shirts, swarmed over the meadow.

'Oh my godfathers!' Sierra slid to a stop in front of Elly as she took in the view. Elly ploughed into her and they clung to each other, giggling as they struggled to keep their balance.

'Come on! Don't start messing around when we've nearly caught them!' Tash pointed. 'There they are!'

Elly looked and her heart thudded with excitement as she spotted five people approaching a barricade on the opposite side of the meadow. A man and a woman in suits, and three figures in hoodies and sunglasses.

'Hurry!' Tash commanded. They sprinted down the last of the hill until they reached the fence. Elly ran as fast as she could as they followed the curve of the fence. She was in the lead when someone grabbed her arm and pulled her to a stop. It was Sierra.

'Through there, jack rabbit!' Sierra pointed back to a narrow gap in the fence that Elly hadn't noticed. Tash was squeezing through, Mojo at her heels. Elly hesitated. Was this trespassing?

'My mum owns the meadow,' Tash called back, seeing her hesitate. 'It's OK. Come on, or they'll disappear before we can find out who they are!' Elly nodded, and squeezed through after Tash. It would be horrible if

they lost them now
after seeing them
land on the island.
On this side of the fence
the noise was even louder: voices shouting, the
thudding of hammers, the whining of drills.
And over it all, the squeals and groans of the
sound system as the technicians continued to
adjust it.

They wove between tents, dodged behind
the portaloos, and crept across the few empty
spaces, stepping over cables, piles of timber
and abandoned tools.

'What a mess!' Sierra said. 'They'll never be
ready for tomorrow.'

'I bet they will.' Elly looked around her. All
the activity, the tension in the air, the noise,
reminded her of the times she'd visited her
mother on set when she was acting in films.
'You'd be surprised how quickly it all comes
together at the end. It only looks messy.'

'It *is* messy. Oh yuck! I don't believe it:

they haven't cleaned up the cowpats! I nearly stepped in that.'

'It's only a cowpat, Sierra. There are worse things . . . ' Tash grabbed the outraged Sierra by the arm and tugged her behind a tent. 'Look!' she hissed.

Elly had spotted them too. Three hooded figures rounded the side of a large tent just ahead of them and disappeared through the entrance.

Tash turned to them, eyes sparkling. 'OK, surveillance team, into position!'

This really is just like a spy film, Elly thought, as she crept to the side of the tent entrance and tried to melt invisibly into the canvas. Tash and Sierra took up positions beside her. Tash was holding Mojo, fishing a treat out of her pocket to bribe him to silence. Oh please

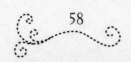

let Mojo behave
himself! Elly felt
her heart thud
faster. It would be a
disaster if he started to
bark now.

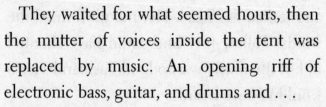

They waited for what seemed hours, then
the mutter of voices inside the tent was
replaced by music. An opening riff of
electronic bass, guitar, and drums and . . .

Elly couldn't believe it! She felt Sierra
jerk with surprise and saw Tash's mouth fall
open. The song flooding out of the tent was
'All Together Now'! The song they were
singing for the festival. And . . . Elly listened
as the vocals started: the clear alto of the lead
singer swelling, leading the two sopranos.
Only one band sounded like that. But she
had to be sure.

Elly edged away from the spellbound
Tash and Sierra. She began to circle the
tent, searching for a way in, and found she

was humming along to the music. There! Her heart gave a skip of joy. A gap where the tent wall hung loosely, flapping slightly in the breeze. This section hadn't been tied in properly. Elly darted back to her friends. She tugged on their arms to get their attention and jerked her head. Her mouth formed the words: Follow me! She could have shouted it, but the music was so loud Tash and Sierra wouldn't have heard.

Sierra's eyes widened at the sight of the loose tent flap. She looked scared but excited. Tash nodded her approval. Elly dropped to her hands and knees and lifted the flap slowly, carefully. She took a deep breath and eased her head and shoulders beneath the flap. As she peered through a haze of electric light and shadow towards the three people playing

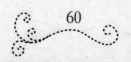

and singing on the stage, her breath escaped in a whoosh of delight.

Even though she had expected to see them, it was still as if someone had given her an electric shock. The Sparks, hoodies and sunglasses discarded, stood at their instruments. Abi was singing, her eyes closed, her hands fluttering over her keyboard like swift-winged birds. Lou sat at her drum kit, chanting the chorus, head swaying, arms flailing as she rapped out the compelling beat. And Marina . . . Elly gasped, then began to breathe again as she saw her favourite singer standing only a few metres away, strumming chords on her electric guitar as she sang. Oh wow, Elly thought, she's amazing.

Elly felt Sierra and Tash squeeze up close on either side of her, but she hardly noticed. She couldn't take her eyes off Marina.

Suddenly, the drum beat faltered and stopped. The music crashed to a halt. Abi slumped at the keyboard. Shrugged. Gazed off into the distance as though, Elly thought, she was pretending not to be there. Marina cocked her head at the drummer.

'What's up, Lou?'

'This isn't working for me,' Lou said. 'You're not keeping to the rhythm, Marina. I'm the drummer. I set the pace. You need to follow me. Is that a problem?'

'Why should it be a problem?' Marina spoke quietly and slowly. Too slowly. Tension was in her voice and suddenly the whole tent seemed full of it, as though the air was charged with electricity.

In the silence, Mojo whined. Tash shushed him frantically. Had the band heard? But Marina and Lou continued to

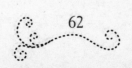

stare at each other, and Abi still gazed into the distance. What's going on? Elly watched the band in dismay. They were supposed to be best friends, these three. It was one of the legends about The Sparks. Maybe this was just how musicians worked. Was this only about the music?

'You tell me why it's a problem now,' Lou answered. She returned Marina's gaze, her face impassive.

Mojo whimpered more loudly, despite Tash's cuddles and whispered pleas for him to be quiet. He doesn't like this argument either, Elly thought. At least The Sparks seemed too caught up in their quarrel to notice the noise of an unhappy little dog.

'Look, can we just get on with it? We've got a concert tomorrow,' Abi broke in. Her voice was tired. 'Once more from the top, OK?

Come on, we know how to do this. Feel the song, guys.'

'Like we used to.' Lou hit a sudden roll on the snare, then set up a slow beat on the bass drum, soft and steady as a ticking clock. 'Together, right? That's what it was always supposed to be about. So keep to the beat, Marina. Unless you've got better things to do.'

'You know I haven't.' Marina's voice was so soft Elly almost couldn't hear the words. Then the singer lifted her head and strummed the opening chords to 'All Together Now', her face frowning in concentration.

At the same moment, someone tapped Elly's ankle. Who had done that? She glanced over her shoulder and saw two pairs of grown-up, official-looking shoes. Sierra gasped and began to scoot backwards.

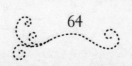

Tash had already disappeared. Elly back-pedalled out of the tent on hands and knees, her heart in her throat.

She emerged from beneath the tent flap into glaring sunshine and squinted up at two frowning security guards. Uh oh! Elly jumped to her feet, smoothing her hair down and brushing her clothes. She felt her face grow hot.

'Oh my godfathers . . .' Sierra muttered, as she staggered to her feet beside Elly. Tash was already standing up, Mojo in her arms. Her face was pink.

'Hi,' she said. 'I'm Natasha Blake-Reynolds. My family own the Meadows and I'm just here making sure everything's going all right for the festival.' Her face grew redder as the security guards, a man and a woman in fluorescent tabards, continued to frown at them.

'Good afternoon, Miss Blake-Reynolds,' the

woman said at last. 'Your family may own the site, but it was rented to the festival for the duration. Which means you're trespassing. This is serious. The festival wants the headline act kept secret and you kids—'

'We won't tell. Promise!' Elly's stomach was twisting in knots. Would Aunt Dina understand that they hadn't meant to trespass? And . . . Oh no! What if The Sparks found out they'd been spying on them? Elly groaned as she imagined Marina staring at her, the singer's face stern with anger and disapproval.

'We really do promise,' Sierra chimed in. 'Cross our hearts and hope to turn into pickled pineapples!' Her grin faded at the sight of the guards' unsmiling faces.

'My mother is one of the festival organizers,' Tash blurted. 'She'd be furious with me if we told. We wouldn't dare. Really!'

'Hmmm . . .' The woman guard glanced at her companion, who shrugged. 'All right. If you kids promise to make yourselves scarce and not come back until the festival opens, we'll forget we saw you today. Deal?'

Tash nodded.

'We swear!' Sierra added fervently. 'We'll be good.'

'Excellent,' the man smiled at last. 'Come on, girls. We'll escort you to the entrance and you can come back tomorrow when the festival is properly open.' He reached down and patted Mojo, who wagged his tail.

'Traitor,' muttered Tash, as they followed the guards out of the festival grounds and the barricade swung shut behind them.

Chapter 6

It was a long, hot walk back up the hill to Sunday House. Mojo scampered ahead of them, seeming totally unaware of the trouble he'd landed them in.

'They won't tell my mother, will they?' Tash asked for the fifth time.

'No, worry wart,' Sierra said. 'We were let off with a caution. Forget it and concentrate on the fact that we saw The Sparks in real life! And we know who the mystery act is before anyone else. And now that we've watched how the pros do it, let's get to work on our performance so we can win *Tomorrow's Stars*.'

'Oh,' Elly sighed, the last of her embarrassment fading as she thought about what it would mean if they won the talent show. 'I'd give anything to meet The Sparks.'

'Right,' Tash said, sounding her cheerful self once more. 'We need to get practising if we're going to get through the auditions tomorrow. Just think how cool it will be if we get to perform at the same festival as The Sparks!'

Sierra grinned at Elly. 'Someone's got stardust in her eyes.'

Elly nodded. Tash's new enthusiasm was great. It had been so exciting being on the festival site. The possibility of actually performing there now seemed real, rather than just a fantasy. 'We'll have to work hard,' she warned. 'Just like The Sparks were doing. They must have performed that song thousands of

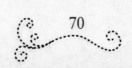

times and they're still working at making it better.'

'I'll work!' Tash promised. 'Come on!' And she broke into a run, sprinting the last hundred metres up the path to Sunday House.

Elly followed. Mostly, she felt excited and happy. But a shadow remained: she hoped she was right and the argument between The Sparks had just been about the music. She just couldn't shake the feeling that something else had been going on.

Elly opened her eyes to bright morning sunshine streaming through her attic bedroom window. Today is the first morning of the festival! The thought jerked her up and out of bed as though she was on puppet strings. This afternoon the first act would appear on the main stage. Would she, Tash, and Sierra be playing at the festival themselves? Only if they got through the first round of *Tomorrow's Stars*. Her stomach twisted with nerves and her throat went dry as she thought about the auditions rushing towards her.

She sang 'All Together Now' as she had a quick shower and dressed. Then she scampered downstairs, drawn by the smell of bacon and eggs. Aunt Dina was already seated at the kitchen table, reading a newspaper. She looked up as Elly entered and waved the paper at her.

'I know who's headlining at the Sunday Island Festival. How much will you pay me for the news?'

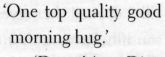

'One top quality good morning hug.'

'Done!' Aunt Dina hugged her back and handed over the newspaper. 'Front page news in the *Sunday*

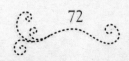

Island Gazette:
it's your favourite
band, The Sparks.
Are you happy?'

Elly grinned at her aunt.
'Amazing!' she said. 'I'm totally happy.' She
hoped Aunt Dina couldn't see she'd known
already. She didn't feel like explaining their
reconnaissance mission to the festival site
yesterday.

She piled her plate high with bacon,
scrambled eggs, and toast. But as soon as
she put the first bite in her mouth her throat
closed up and she could barely swallow. Elly
choked and took a sip of orange juice. Then
she stared at her plate. Suddenly she didn't
feel very hungry.

'Nerves?' Aunt Dina was smiling at her
across the table.

'I can't remember the words to the song!'
Elly said, panic fluttering in her chest. Her
mind had gone blank. But she was the lead

 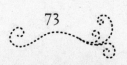

singer. She couldn't let Tash and Sierra down.

'You're enough of a pro to know about stage fright, Elly.' Aunt Dina pointed to the photograph on the wall above the table. It showed the whole family: Gran, Mum, Dad, Aunt Dina, and a very much younger Elly. Elly looked at it and the familiar pain throbbed for a moment in her chest. How she wished she could talk to Mum right now. Before her death from cancer a few months ago, her mother had spent years working as an actress. She would have understood how Elly was feeling.

'You are your mother's daughter, love,' Aunt Dina continued. 'You'll be all right on the night.'

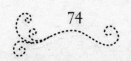

'Hmm.' Elly's eyes didn't leave the photo. She gazed at her mother's smiling, happy face. She wouldn't let Mum down.

'I guess,' Elly said.
'Only the audition
isn't tonight, it's
this morning!'

'See you there.' Aunt
Dina grinned at her. 'Don't forget, my band's
auditioning too.'

Elly bit her lip. Oh dear! 'Good luck,'
she said, trying to keep the doubt out of her
voice. Perhaps a miracle would happen and
Aunt Dina would somehow manage to sing
in tune. 'But remember,' she said, 'I'll love
you no matter what.'

Aunt Dina looked startled. 'That bad, is it?'
She raised an eyebrow as Elly spluttered a
denial. Her aunt chuckled. 'It's fine, love. By
Apollo, the nine Muses, and the be-wigged
genius that was Bach, I know I can't carry a
tune. But I still like singing, and the others
don't seem to mind. We're just having a bit of
fun. My money's on you girls, to be honest.'

Elly managed to eat a bit more breakfast,

then said goodbye to Aunt Dina and headed over to the caravan site. They were meeting at Sierra's to get ready. Sierra had organized everything, insisting on being in charge of make-up and costumes. Elly had no idea what she would be wearing for the audition.

The caravan door crashed open before she could even knock. A flustered Sierra grabbed her by the wrist and pulled her inside. 'Would you please come and tell Tash that I know what I'm doing!'

Oh no! Elly rolled her eyes. This wasn't a good start.

Sierra pushed open the door to her bedroom and a riot of colour and chaos met Elly's eyes. Clothes were strewn across bed, chair and floor. Shoes, make-up, pots of nail varnish and cans of spray-on hair colour littered every surface. And in the centre of it all stood Tash. Elly blinked in astonishment. 'Tash!' she gasped. 'You look fabulous!'

Tash's short blonde hair was styled into a softly spiked look, with feathers of hair framing her eyes and ears. Someone had artfully painted pink and purple streaks through the blonde locks. She wore dangling glittery purple earrings, sparkling green nail varnish on her short fingernails, a mini-skirt with leggings underneath and a short, boxy purple sequinned jacket. On her feet, in total contrast, were acid-green lace-up trainers. Tash had firmly refused to dance in heels. Mojo was sniffing the green shoes suspiciously.

'Do you think so?' Tash frowned at herself in the full length mirror. 'I do like the trainers, but I feel like an idiot in this skirt. I *never* wear skirts!'

'She won't let me do the make-up,' Sierra

complained, following Elly into the room and standing with her hands on her hips, staring accusingly at the unrepentant Tash. 'See? Elly has just confirmed my genius. Why can't you just trust me? I'm the fashion diva here.'

Tash wrinkled her nose in distaste. 'Lipstick and eyeliner make me feel like a clown.'

'Well of course,' Elly said, 'it would be totally weird to wear it all the time. But this is a performance. It's like the make-up you wear for a play. Otherwise, no one will be able to see your face when you're on stage.'

'Oh all right,' Tash grumbled. 'But you two go first.'

Sierra shrugged. 'Fine. I'm dying to get Elly dressed up. Look what I've got for you! Our lead singer is going to knock 'em dead.'

Sierra held up a long, silky tunic embroidered with green and gold sequins.

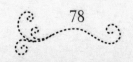

It shimmered as the light struck it.

'Wow! Where do you get these things?' Elly asked. The tunic was gorgeous, and the colour would look great with her curly black hair.

'My mum is totally obsessed with clothes.'

'Wonder who you take after then,' muttered Tash.

Sierra ignored her. 'And she gives me loads of stuff when she's bored with it. I'm lucky because this year we're nearly the same size.' She held up dark gold leggings and a handful of gold bangles. 'Let's get you dressed, then.'

Half an hour later, Elly stared at herself in the mirror, entranced. Sierra had dry-waxed and brushed her hair until it rayed away from her head like a soft, black cloud. Then she had painted on black and gold hair glitter and applied gold eye shadow. Elly wore big gold hoop earrings and bangles on both arms, and her nails were painted black, with glittering gold crescent moons on each nail. Beside the tunic and leggings, she wore knee-high black boots Sierra had somehow managed to find in a charity shop. They were a perfect fit.

'How did you know my shoe size?'

'Remember the flip-flops? I've known your shoe size for ages.' Sierra grinned at her, obviously pleased with her handiwork. 'You really look good, Elly. You look like your mum, actually, with your hair like that. You know, the photo in your bedroom.'

Elly nodded, her throat too tight to speak. She'd been thinking the same thing. She did look like her mum and that was both a sad and a happy feeling. 'You'd better get into costume too,' she managed to say. Sierra dressed with quick efficiency.

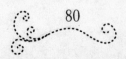

'She's done this before,' Tash said drily, watching Sierra slip into black skinny jeans with black sequins zigzagging up the seams, and a hot-pink silk shirt. Sierra slipped her feet into raspberry-coloured leather shoes with glittery toes and three-inch killer heels.

'Can you really dance in those?' Tash asked. 'I couldn't even walk in them!'

''Course I can. I dance in heels all the time. I'm training to be a professional, remember?'

'Well, you're already miles taller than me,' Tash grumbled. 'And I'm wearing flats.'

'Oh, poor little baby bear.' Sierra grinned at Tash. 'But you have the coolest trainers in town, so no one will care that you're vertically challenged.'

Tash grabbed a cushion from the bed and threw it at Sierra, who ducked with a laugh.

Mojo growled in delight and attacked the

cushion, biting one corner and tugging it, trying to pick it up.

'It's bigger than you are, silly dog!' Tash said with a giggle, rescuing the cushion.

'No pillow fights,' Elly said, her stomach lurching as she checked her watch. 'We need to get going.'

'Help!' screamed Sierra. 'I haven't done my hair or Tash's make-up yet!'

There was last minute madness as Elly helped Sierra paint pink glitter strands in her long dark hair, then soothed Tash as Sierra applied lip gloss and eye shadow to their reluctant friend. Finally, Elly draped an arm around them both and whirled them all around for a last look in the mirror.

'What do you reckon?' Elly asked. She smiled at their reflection, her nerves

almost forgotten. 'I
think we look great.
And that'll make us
sing great too.'

'Wow,' Tash said. 'I take it
back, Sierra. You're a genius. We look like a
proper band.'

Mojo barked his agreement.

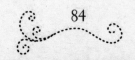

Chapter 7

Elly's nerves had returned full force by the time they reached the Town Hall, where the auditions were being held. A long queue of contestants for *Tomorrow's Stars* reached from the front door down the steps, onto the pavement and around the corner. There were people of all ages, from grandads to kids hardly out of nursery school.

'Oh my godfathers!' Sierra exclaimed as they joined the end of the queue. 'Who knew there'd be so many people auditioning? Rats! My feet are killing me.'

Tash raised an eyebrow. 'Take the heels off

till we get inside,' she advised, picking Mojo up to keep him from making friends with the entire queue.

Sierra nodded and grabbed hold of Elly's shoulder while she slipped the glittery pink shoes off. 'Oh,' she groaned. 'That's way better. Who invented these things?'

'I thought you danced in heels all the time?' Tash smirked. She was trying to fasten a lead onto her border terrier's collar. 'Stop wriggling!'

'I'm not! Oh…you meant Mojo,' Sierra said. Elly dissolved into giggles and Sierra turned to her with a frown. 'Hey, it's an honest mistake. And I do dance in heels, Tash, it's just that my dance shoes are way comfier than these.'

'Look!' Elly jumped up and down with excitement. 'There's Aunt

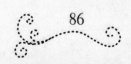

Dina. And your
mum, Tash. And
your dad, Sierra.'

Their adults were
standing halfway up the
queue. Aunt Dina glanced back and
spotted Elly waving. She was wearing her
seventies get up, but Elly was too happy to see
her to care. Aunt Dina strode towards them,
her maxi dress flowing behind her.

'Elly! Girls!' Aunt Dina beamed at them.
'You three look fabulous. Absolutely stunning.'
She smiled at Sierra. 'Well done. You should
win on costumes alone.'

'Oh thank you!' Sierra blushed through her
make-up. 'And you look . . . well, you've really
got the retro seventies thing going there . . . '
her voice trailed away, and Aunt Dina threw
her head back and roared with laughter.

'Next time I'll book you as our fashion
consultant, Miss Cruz.' She kissed Elly on
the cheek. 'Good luck, you three!' Then she

returned to her place in the queue. Sierra's dad and Mrs Blake-Reynolds waved at them, but didn't come to talk to them, which made Elly rather relieved. They looked even odder than Aunt Dina, who seemed able to carry off anything she wore, no matter how bizarre.

'Oh, I hope they don't do too badly . . .' Sierra frowned at her father pensively. 'He's actually a very good musician, but this isn't really his style of music.'

'They'll be fine,' Tash said. 'After all, they don't care if they meet The Sparks or not. It's just a bit of fun for them.' She sighed. 'I don't feel so well. My stomach's gone all squirmy.' Mojo whimpered in sympathy and licked her chin.

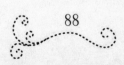

Elly gave Tash's hand a quick squeeze. She was feeling a bit light-headed herself. Act after

act disappeared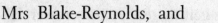
through the door,
and soon Aunt Dina,
Mrs Blake-Reynolds, and
Mr Cruz had disappeared too. The acts
were being ticked off a list by the large man
with the red face and dark suit guarding the
entrance. 'Stage manager,' Elly said wisely,
trying to comfort herself that she was an old
hand at this performing stuff. The daughter of
a pro; on television herself before she could
even walk. 'Shame I can't remember it,'
she muttered.

'Remember what?' Sierra asked.

Before Elly could explain, the red-faced
man motioned them forward. 'Name?' he
barked.

'Uh, Tash . . . ' Tash said. 'And this is Elly
and—'

'No!' He glared at them, a bead of sweat
dripping down his nose. 'Not your names!
The name of the act.'

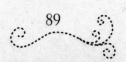

Elly's eyes widened. How could they have forgotten to give themselves a name? They had to come up with something fast. The man's face was getting redder and crosser. He glared at them impatiently.

Elly's brain went blank and her throat dry. She put her hand up to her neck and her fingers touched cool smooth metal: the chain holding her mother's pendant. The friendship charms!

'Have you girls got a name or not? If you don't then you'll have to—'

'It's this!' Elly cried. She pulled her silver charm out of the neck of her costume and brandished it at Tash and 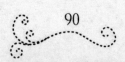 Sierra, watching their faces change from shock and horror to relief. The charms were the symbols of their friendship: the silver tokens they had

inherited from
their mothers
and which had
helped them solve
the first mystery of their
summer together on Sunday Island.

'Yeah!' Sierra shot her armful of bangles into the air: the silver charm on her bracelet shone in the sunlight. 'It's The Charms!'

'The Charms!' Tash agreed, touching the silver badge she had pinned to the neck of her jacket. 'That's us.'

The man huffed, and wrote it down. 'Right. Inside and wait in the corridor with the other acts. You'll be given a call when it's time to go on. Listen up for it. You miss the call, you miss your slot. And mind that dog doesn't . . .'

But they had already pushed through the door out of earshot. They walked down a long passage and through another door into a long room full of nervous people. Mojo whined and wriggled harder in Tash's arms. 'He wants to explore,' Tash said, keeping a firm grip on her dog as she followed Elly and Sierra into the centre of the room. 'Be a good boy, Mojo. Mum will look after you while we perform.'

From time to time, a woman with a clipboard came through another door further up the hall and called out three acts. Every time, the low level buzz of voices broke off anxiously, and the performers who'd been called filed out of the hall after her.

Elly looked around. No sign of Aunt Dina or the others. They must have already been called. Her stomach squirmed again.

Sierra pulled her heels back on. Her eyes were sparkling and she looked excited and happy. Elly noticed that Tash looked anything but happy. If Elly was nervous, Tash must be feeling ten times worse. Elly wanted to

be an actress like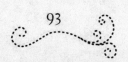
her mother. She
performed in school
plays and went to stage
school on Saturdays. Tash had probably never
done anything like this before.

'You look really great,' Elly whispered to
her friend, giving her hand a quick squeeze.
Tash grinned weakly and looked a bit less
nervous. 'This is going to be fun,' Elly said.
'Just pretend we're back in your bedroom
practising. We're going to knock 'em out!'

Tash nodded, colour coming back into
her face.

'Good luck, girls!' Mrs Blake-Reynolds
pushed through the crowd towards them,
trailed by Mr Cruz and Aunt Dina. 'It's up
to you now: family honour and all that.' She
smiled as she took Mojo's lead from Tash. 'I
think I'm supposed to tell you to break a leg,
Natasha, but I'd rather you didn't.'

'Oh.' Elly's smile faded as she looked at

Aunt Dina. 'You didn't get through?'

''Fraid not.' Aunt Dina shrugged. 'One of the judges gave us the thumbs up, but then had the cheek to say it was for our sheer bravery in performing in public!' But she grinned and Elly knew she didn't really mind.

Mr Cruz kissed Sierra on the hand, gallantly. '*Chicas hermosas!* You are visions of loveliness, you girls. You win for us. I only wish we could watch you perform, but only judges allowed, I'm afraid.'

'The Charms! Calling The Charms!' The woman with the clipboard had appeared at the door again. Elly's heart gave a jerking leap.

'Oh help!' Tash squealed.

'Come on!' Sierra grabbed Elly and Tash by the arms and towed them towards the door. 'Fame awaits!'

Two minutes later they were standing on stage,

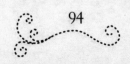

spotlights shining in their faces, looking out at the vague shapes of the three judges sitting in the darkened auditorium.

Elly stood between Tash and Sierra, holding their hands.

'The Charms!' a voice announced, and then the introductory chords of 'All Together Now' began to play over the sound system. Elly pushed down a surge of pure panic and, as she knew it would, all the practice they'd done came to her rescue. She took up her position, nodding her head to the beat and, right on cue, her clear alto soared above the backing track. Sierra and Tash joined in. She took a moment to feel relieved that Tash's voice was strong and accurate as ever, and then every thought was swallowed by concentration as the dancing and singing began in earnest.

They were halfway through the routine

when disaster struck: Tash stumbled and stopped dancing. Distracted, Elly staggered to a halt. Without missing a beat, Sierra shimmied in front of Elly and Tash and led the dance routine. With her to follow, Elly found it easy to get the steps back, and Tash seemed to recover just as well. Elly's heart was beating with relief as well as exertion as they sang the final chorus and struck the final pose.

They'd done it! Not as well as they'd managed in rehearsal, but they had done their best. The only question remaining was, would that be good enough?

Elly stood, panting, heart thudding with anxiety, and stared out at the judges. The house lights brightened and now she could see the three people they'd been performing for. Two women and a man. Not smiling at all! Elly felt Sierra and then Tash reach out and take her by the hand. Had they blown it after all? Had they failed to get through the first stage of *Tomorrow's Stars*? Elly felt sick with apprehension.

The judge on the left, an older woman, smiled at last and put her thumb up. 'Well done,' she called.

Elly's eyes turned to the next judge. Her heart was pounding in her ears and she could feel sweat dripping down her forehead. This judge was a man, small and slightly plump, with ridiculously large spectacles. He shrugged, shot out his hand and slowly turned his thumb . . . up!

The last judge frowned, glanced at her notes, then nodded. She put out a manicured hand and turned one elegant red-nailed thumb to point at the ceiling. 'You're through the first round,' she called. 'You'll be playing the festival in the small tent tonight with the other finalists. Congratulations, Charms. And good recovery,' she called to Sierra. 'Nicely done.' And she, too, smiled.

Elly screamed. So did Tash and Sierra. They hugged, thanked the judges, and staggered offstage and out into the summer sunshine. They had done it!

Chapter 8

Their grown-ups were waiting for them outside the hall. Aunt Dina took one look at Elly's happy face and whooped with joy. 'Yes!' She gave them each a big, squashy Aunt Dina hug. 'I'm so proud of you three. I can't wait to see you perform tonight.'

'Are you all right, Natasha?' Mrs Blake-Reynolds handed over Mojo's lead then stood back to study her daughter. 'I could tell you were nervous. I want you to know how very proud I am that you went ahead and performed.' Tash grinned and hugged her mother. Mojo barked until Tash scooped him up into the hug as well.

Mr Cruz was holding Sierra's hand. In her heels she was inches taller than her dad. 'I can't believe this grown-up young lady is my little tearaway.' He smiled at her fondly. 'I too cannot wait to see the three of you perform tonight. But you haven't heard the latest gossip!'

'What?' Elly could tell Sierra's dad was bursting to tell them something important.

'The headlining band, The Sparks, have disappeared!' he announced.

'Disappeared?' Elly stared at him, stunned. 'What do you mean?'

'Have they been kidnapped? Are they being held for ransom by evil criminals?' Sierra's eyes grew round as she took in the news. Tash was frowning with worry.

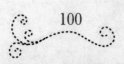

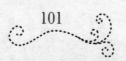

'It's the talk of the town,' Aunt Dina said. 'They were supposed to be here now, to be officially introduced as the headlining band and to announce the names of the *Tomorrow's Stars* finalists over the Town Hall loudspeaker. But it seems they haven't shown up.'

'Which means the Lord Mayor will do the announcing.' Mrs Blake-Reynolds gave an exasperated sigh. 'She's delighted, of course. Miriam does so love the sound of her own voice.'

'I'm sorry,' Aunt Dina said, patting Elly on the shoulder. 'I know you would have loved seeing your favourite band in person and having them announce you girls as one of the finalists.'

'But what's happened to them?' Elly pushed her disappointment away.

'I expect they're just tired; or hiding from

all the paparazzi,' Tash said. 'Sunday Island is crawling with photographers. In case you hadn't noticed, we've had our photos taken about five times in the last few minutes.' She put Mojo on the ground, holding firmly onto his lead, and pointed to the town square, where several photographers stood like islands in a human sea, clicking away as the crowd parted to flow around them.

'Oh, great!' Sierra straightened up, flicked her long hair over her shoulder and waved at the photographers. 'Do you think they know we're finalists?'

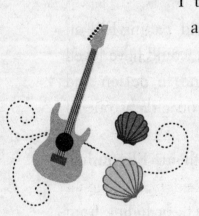

'I think they're doing what are called candid shots of the crowd,' Mrs Blake-Reynolds said. 'But you'll be getting your pictures in the *Sunday Island Gazette* later today. It's running a story on *Tomorrow's Stars*

and the finalists.'

'Whoopee!' Sierra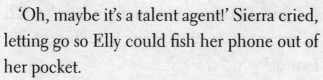
shrieked, hugging
Tash and Elly. 'Fame!'

Elly's phone rang.

'Oh, maybe it's a talent agent!' Sierra cried,
letting go so Elly could fish her phone out of
her pocket.

Her heart chugged into high gear when she
saw who was calling. 'It's my dad!' she cried.
She took a deep breath and punched the
receive button. 'Dad?'

'Hi, Sweetie.' She could just make out the
words over the sounds of the busy festival
town. It was so fabulous to hear his voice,
especially right now. 'So?' he said. 'Don't
keep me in suspense. How'd you do?'

'You are talking to one of *Tomorrow's Stars*.
We made it! We're one of the finalists.'

'I'm so proud of you.' Dad sounded as if he
was choking up. Elly grinned: he was such a
softie. 'Your mother would be proud too.'

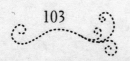

Now it was Elly's turn to feel a lump in her throat.

'Elly, I'm coming to see you.'

'What?' She swallowed the lump. Had she heard right?

'I said, I'm coming down from London. I'll be there tomorrow to see you perform at the festival.'

'But ... we might not win. We're performing tonight with all the other finalists, but I can't promise we'll be the ones to make it to the main stage.'

'I just have a feeling, Elly. But whether you're on the main stage or not, I'll be there tomorrow and we can enjoy the last night of the festival together. Ask Dina to record your performance tonight so I can see it. Whatever happens, I'm so proud of you. Just

give it your best shot, and you'll be fine. No one can do more. Gotta go now. Love you.'

'Love you . . . ' Elly lowered the phone. 'Dad's coming,' she told Aunt Dina. 'He asked if you could record our act tonight.'

'Mobile charged and ready,' Aunt Dina said. 'Did he say when he's arriving?'

'Just tomorrow.' The news was starting to seep into her brain, and Elly hugged herself with happiness. She hadn't seen her father for weeks. She had so much news to tell him, and so much to show him. And she especially wanted to introduce him to her best friends.

'I can't wait to meet your dad,' Sierra cried. 'It's so great he can come to watch us perform.'

'I bet he'll love the tree house,' Tash said. 'We can take him sailing!'

'I expect he'll only be here for a day or two,' Aunt Dina warned.

'Now, what are you girls going to do between now and this evening's performance?' Tash's mum asked. 'You need to get out of those costumes, for a start, so they don't get ruined.'

Elly nodded. 'And then we're going to practise the act.'

'What?' Tash cried. 'But . . . '

'My dad is coming,' Elly said. 'I want him to see us on that main stage.'

'Me too,' Sierra agreed. 'We need to practise the dance again.'

'That was my fault.' Tash slumped. 'I'm just not good enough.'

'Rubbish,' Sierra said briskly. 'You just need a bit more practice and a lot more confidence.'

'I know,' Elly cried. 'After we change, let's go and talk to Dorothy and ask for a few more pointers. She was so helpful yesterday.'

'Great idea!' Sierra said. Tash nodded in agreement.

Dorothy's face lit up in a bright smile when she opened the door and saw them standing on her front step. 'How did the audition go?' she asked.

'We did it! We got through the first round!' Sierra and Elly cried together.

'And there's a mystery,' Tash added. 'The Sparks are missing!'

'They were supposed to be at the auditions today and announce the acts that got through the first round,' Elly explained. 'But they didn't show up. I'm really worried they won't sing at the festival!'

Dorothy's expression changed from smile to frown. 'We'll just have to hope that everything will work out for the best,' she said. 'I admit I had heard something about this already.' She sighed and Elly thought she suddenly looked very sad. But the next moment her frown lifted and she smiled at each of them in turn. 'But the important thing is that you girls got through the auditions!'

'Thanks to you,' Tash said.

'Nonsense.' Dorothy shook her head. 'You girls worked hard and you deserve your success. I'm so pleased for you. And it's an especially nice surprise that you've dropped by today,' she continued. 'Because I've got a surprise for you. Please come in.'

Dorothy bustled down the hall in front of them and pushed open the sitting room door, a mysterious smile hovering on her lips. 'I'd like you to meet my granddaughter, Em. I've told her all about you girls.'

Elly followed Sierra and Tash inside then froze.

Her eyes widened and she felt her mouth drop open. It couldn't be! There, standing next to the mantelpiece and looking at the photograph of herself as a girl, was Marina, lead singer of The Sparks.

Em . . . Elly's brain clicked into gear despite the shock and her eyes flicked from Marina's face to the mantelpiece. That's why the girl in the photo had looked somehow familiar! She'd thought 'Em' had been short for Emily or Emma. But actually it was just the letter 'M'. M for Marina. The lead singer of The Sparks was Dorothy's granddaughter!

Chapter 9

'Oh my great-uncles, great-aunts, and godfathers,' Sierra gasped. 'I think I'm going to die!'

'Don't do that!' Marina had been looking sad but now her eyes twinkled just like her grandmother's. 'Think of all the problems figuring out what to put on the death certificate. Spontaneous combustion? Death by celebrity? A fatal case of fan-itis?' She grinned. 'You've got to be Sierra! And you ...' she pointed at Tash. 'You're Tash, right? Of tree house fame. Which means you must be Elly, the budding actress.' She smiled at them in turn. 'Hi. Gran's told me lots about you guys.'

'Take them into the garden, Em,' Dorothy said. 'I'll bring a bite of lunch out. It's a lovely day and we should make the most of it.'

'Oh, but we can't invite ourselves to lunch.' Tash looked horrified.

'You didn't, Gran did,' Marina said with a smile. 'And I learnt years ago that it's easiest just to do what she tells you. This way.' She led the way out of the hall and through a door into a large back garden filled with flowers. Agapanthus and scented geraniums overflowed from terracotta pots scattered about the weathered stone terrace.

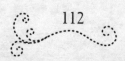

Borders full of climbing roses, clematis, and flowers Elly didn't even recognize filled the air with delicate perfumes.

'Wow,' Elly breathed,

as Marina ushered them to a table and chairs on the terrace. 'This is a beautiful garden.'

'Gran's got green fingers, all right,' Marina said. She flopped into a chair beside Elly. 'It's always so peaceful here. Like a little bit of heaven. I just feel myself relaxing the moment I step through the door.'

Elly glanced at Tash and Sierra. Tash raised an eyebrow. So she'd noticed it too: Marina looked exhausted. Her freckles stood out on her pale skin and her eyes were red-rimmed.

Elly still couldn't believe she was sitting next to her idol. Marina looked so normal too: like anyone's big sister. She was in scruffy jeans and a T-shirt. Her hair looked as if it had just come out of the shower, been combed through and left to dry, and she wasn't wearing a speck of make-up or any jewellery other than a small nose stud. She could walk down the town square right now, Elly thought, filled as it was with festival goers and paparazzi, and no one would ever notice her.

'Did you stay on Sunday Island a lot when you were our age?' Sierra asked.

'Loads!' The strained look left Marina's face and she smiled. 'I couldn't wait to come and stay with Gran and I'm dying to hear what you guys get up to. So come on: what have you been doing all summer?'

'Well, it all started with a treasure hunt and an open grave!' Sierra began.

'And then we got shipwrecked and the whales came!' Elly interrupted, remembering Elly Island, the mother whale and her baby.

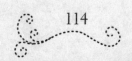

'Don't forget the World War Two tunnels and my grandfather's inventions!' Tash chimed in. 'The ghost-detector worked, no matter what Sierra says.'

'Whoa!' Marina held

both hands up.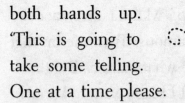
'This is going to
take some telling.
One at a time please.
Let's start at the beginning. Sierra?'

While the girls told her about their
amazing summer, Dorothy served up a lunch
of American-style chicken club sandwiches
on fresh home-made bread and a juicy
tomato, olive, and feta cheese salad. 'You
guys are adventure magnets. I'm so jealous,'
Marina said.

'Jealous?' Sierra spluttered through a
mouthful of chicken. 'You're a famous pop
star. I mean . . . that's way more cool than
having adventures.'

'Is it?' Marina's face grew still. 'I love making
music. It must be the way you feel about your
acting, right, Elly?'

Elly nodded.

'And your dancing, Sierra; and Tash's
sailing. Doing stuff you love is important.

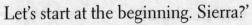

That and friendship.' Marina drew a deep breath. 'Not being famous. Trust me on that one, girls. People are what matters. But this is way too heavy. What I really want to know is: can I visit your tree house?'

'Are you serious?' Sierra squealed. 'Of course!'

'Absolutely!' Tash said, a broad grin of pride on her face.

Elly just smiled at Marina. It felt as if they'd made a new friend.

'Wait till I tell Dad!' Sierra whipped out her mobile and began to text.

'I like your style, Sierra,' Marina said. 'Look at this.' She tugged a phone from her back pocket and held it out. It was bright pink.

'Oh!' Sierra squealed. 'We've got the same phone! I can't believe it. What apps have you got?' The two of them bent over the phones, comparing apps and games as Dorothy appeared with a plate of meringues and fresh raspberries and cream for pudding.

'There goes my diet!' Sierra put down her phone and grabbed her spoon in readiness.

'What diet?' Tash teased. 'You eat more than Elly and me put together.'

'Fast metabolism.' Sierra shrugged. 'I can't help it if I'm meant to eat lots.'

'Performing burns a lot of calories. I'm eating tons on this tour,' Marina said.

Elly realized that they'd spent all lunch talking about themselves. That was rude. And she wanted to hear about Marina's exciting life as a pop star. 'It's so cool that you're headlining the festival tomorrow,' she said. 'Are you excited?'

Marina's face fell. Elly felt awful. Somehow she'd said the wrong thing.

'Actually,' Marina said, with a glance at her grandmother, who was frowning with concern. 'Things aren't going that well at the moment.' She hesitated.

'Are The Sparks having a row?' Sierra blurted. She flushed bright red as Marina turned a surprised face towards her. 'We . . . we sort of overheard you yesterday in the tent . . . it sounded like an argument.'

'The tent! How did you . . . ?' Marina shook her head and laughed. 'After hearing about your adventures I should have guessed that if there was anything at all happening on Sunday Island you guys would be in the thick of it.' She sighed. 'Yeah . . . We used to be so close. Just like you guys. Friends first and for ever. But now . . . ' She frowned, then smiled a bright and, Elly knew, totally fake smile.

'It's OK, really. It'll work out. But I've got to admit I'd much rather hang out with you guys this week than do the festival. Which reminds me . . .' She grabbed her mobile and stared at it. 'Look at the time! I've got to try and find Abi and Lou and squeeze in one more rehearsal.'

'So you are going to perform at the festival after all,' Elly said, hopeful.

'I certainly hope so,' Marina replied. 'We can't disappoint such great fans like you.' She swallowed hard. 'Thanks so much for the lunch, Gran. You are a total star. And girls, lovely to meet you. I'll come and watch you perform tonight—no matter what. What song are you singing?'

'It's—' Elly began.

'It's a secret!' Sierra interrupted.

'What else? Another mystery to solve.' Marina waved goodbye. 'See you tonight

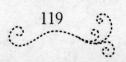

then.' She shoved her phone into her back pocket. Elly felt a strangely sad feeling in her chest as Marina jogged towards the house and disappeared.

Elly turned to Dorothy. 'Thank you for lunch. And for letting us meet Marina. I'm never going to forget today.'

'She's a good girl,' Dorothy said fondly. 'And a hard worker, like you girls. Now, do I guess correctly that you'd like a bit of help with your act before tonight?'

Elly, Tash, and Sierra nodded in unison. 'We'll do the washing up first,' Sierra said, leaping to her feet and gathering plates and cutlery. 'And then yes, please! A lesson would be fabulous!'

Elly stood alone in the garden for a moment, after the others had gone inside. She was thrilled to have

met Marina and
made friends with
her. But what was at
the heart of the argument
between The Sparks? What could possibly
have damaged a legendary friendship? Elly
hoped Marina was right and it would all work
out. But the truth was, she wasn't so sure.

Chapter 10

The weather was being kind to the Sunday Island Music Festival. The sky was cloudless and the breeze had dropped when Elly, Tash, and Sierra left the caravan for Melody Meadows later that afternoon.

They were back in costume, with hair freshly styled, nail varnish retouched, and make-up reapplied. Sierra wore her pink flip-flops and carried her heels in her handbag.

'I think this may be the best day of my life!' She twirled round and round on the path in front of them, her arms flung wide. 'Other than meeting you guys, of course.' She gave one last skip of happiness and fell into step beside them.

'Of course,' Elly said with a giggle. 'Goes without saying.' She looked at Tash, expecting her friend to join in the fun, but Tash didn't look like she was enjoying herself. Uh oh, thought Elly. She had hoped the session with Dorothy would have calmed Tash's nerves, but it looked as if they were back stronger than ever. Tash's face was pale and her eyes fixed on the ground.

Elly nudged Sierra and jerked her head towards the silent Tash. Sierra's smile faded and a worried frown grew in its place.

'Tash,' Elly said. 'Are you all right?'

'I wish Mojo was here,' Tash muttered, still not looking at them. 'He's my lucky charm.'

'You know he can't come with us tonight,' Sierra said. 'And you have us.'

'I know.' Tash sighed.

'How are you feeling about performing?' Elly asked.

'Awful.' Tash looked up at them at last. She bit her lip, and Elly could see she was struggling not to cry. 'I'm really nervous. I'm not sure I can do this.'

'But you've already done it!' Sierra said. 'You did it in front of the judges.'

'And that was hard enough.' Tash tugged at her hair, messing up Sierra's careful arranging. 'I really don't want to let you guys down, but it's one thing to perform in front of three judges. It's totally different to get on stage in front of hundreds of people who have paid actual money to see you. I'm terrified I'm going to mess up again.'

'And if you do, we'll sort it. Just like we did last time. But you won't!' Sierra hugged Tash, then quickly re-arranged her hair. 'You're brilliant. Just believe in yourself. Stop thinking and just do it. And remember we're here for you.'

'Friends for ever!' Elly said. She grabbed Tash and Sierra by the hand. 'It doesn't matter what happens tonight, Tash. What matters is our friendship. And now I think we should forget all about the performance and just have some fun at the festival. Aunt Dina gave me some spending money and I'm starving.'

'So am I,' Sierra said. She sniffed the air. Melody Meadows had just come in sight, banners and flags flying; loudspeakers blaring out music. And beneath it all, like the hum of a beehive, the mutter of hundreds of happy festival goers. 'I detect doughnuts at fifty paces.'

Tash burst into laughter and they were all still giggling as they joined the queue to get into the festival.

Elly felt like a proper VIP

when she displayed her pass to get in free as a *Tomorrow's Stars* finalist. The man on the gate congratulated them and promised to come and hear them sing.

Sierra beamed as the people behind them began to tell everyone that some finalists were queuing just ahead of them. 'It's like we're famous,' she whispered.

'Famous or not, I'm starving,' Elly interrupted. 'Where are these doughnuts of yours?'

Fifteen minutes later, laden down with fizzy drinks and a bag of sugary jam doughnuts, still warm from the fryer, the girls wandered round the festival grounds, twisting between tents and tourists, listening to snatches of music broadcast from every point of the compass, peering into tents to watch bands they'd never heard of before and some they had, chomping doughnuts and singing along.

When the doughnuts were gone, they made their way over to the patch of meadow which formed an open air dance floor. Two giant screens broadcast the bands playing on the main stage and enormous loudspeakers blared music. The dance area was crammed with festival goers of all ages, shapes, and sizes dancing or just bopping up and down to the beat.

'Let's have a go!' Sierra cried, pulling Elly and Tash into the crowd. Soon they were following Sierra's lead and copying, or trying to copy her moves as she shimmied and swayed to the music. Before long, even Tash had a wide grin on her face. Good, thought Elly, she's forgotten to be nervous.

Then they all had something else to think

about. A loud crash
of thunder boomed
overhead. All the
dancers stopped as though
choreographed. They stared up at the sky just
as the heavens opened and rain poured down
in drenching sheets. One of Sunday Island's
freak storms had joined the party.

There were screams of shock followed by
cries of delight as the thunder stopped and the
deluge turned into a steady shower. The cool
rain felt delicious after the August heat and
sunshine and all that dancing. Elly turned
her face up and held out her arms. 'Lovely!'
she cried.

'No!' It was Sierra, and she sounded frantic.

'What's wrong?' Tash and Elly said together,
turning to look at their friend.

'It'll ruin our costumes!' Sierra shrieked.
'Your make-up is getting all smeared, Elly.
Run for cover!'

'Oh fudge!' Elly muttered. She'd been

having so much fun she'd completely forgotten about being in costume. Tash and Sierra were trying to squeeze a way through the crowd of people dancing in the rain. They kept getting blocked or twirled in the wrong direction. Elly followed.

'Excuse us! Please! Let us through!' Sierra bellowed.

But it was no use. No one was listening; the music was blaring and the grass underfoot was rapidly turning to a sea of mud. Someone bumped into Elly and she fell onto her hands and knees. She scrambled up in time to see both Tash and Sierra take a tumble and go sliding on their fronts.

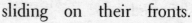

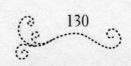

She ran to them and tugged Tash upright. They both reached down and pulled Sierra to her feet.

'My outfit! It's ruined!'

Sierra moaned. 'And I've got mud in my hair.'

'Mud fight!' Shouted someone nearby. And almost as soon as the words had finished, globs of muck were flying through the air.

'No!' Sierra wailed. 'Anyone hits me with a mud ball and I'll . . . I'll . . . ' A sloppy brown lump struck her in the chest and splattered in a star-shape all across her front. Sierra stared down at herself in horror.

Elly couldn't help it. The look on Sierra's face was priceless. She clapped a muddy hand over her mouth, but peals of laughter broke through. Tash took one look at them both and began to giggle. A dark look glinted in Sierra's eye.

'Funny?' she shouted over the noise of the rain and the music. 'You think mud is funny? OK! Have some of your own!' She leaned over and scooped up a handful. 'Mud fight!'

Sierra yelled, and threw the mud ball straight at Elly.

Elly ducked and the mud ball hit Tash—Splat!—in the forehead. Tash's blue eyes shone dangerously through dripping brown muck.

'You're in for it now, Sierra!' Elly shrieked in delight. She scooped up handfuls of mud and flung them rapid fire, first at Sierra, who held her purple handbag in front of her as a shield; then at Tash, who was bending, grabbing mud and throwing with methodical precision. Elly was giggling so hard her aim was rubbish, but so was Sierra's. Tash plastered them both.

Fifteen minutes later, the freak thunderstorm had faded away, the skies had lightened again and the sun broke through to reveal a muddy, happy,

exhausted crowd on the
open air dance floor.

'That was hilarious,'
Tash cried, as the three
of them collapsed in a giggly,
muddy heap. 'The look on your face when
that mud splatted your shirt, Sierra. I'll never
forget it.'

Sierra's happy grin faded as the sunshine
brightened. 'That reminds me. It's nearly time
for our performance. How can we get cleaned
up in time? We can't go onstage like this!' She
fished her phone out of her mud-coloured
handbag and punched buttons frantically.
'Maybe Dad can bring us some clean clothes.
He won't know what to bring but I'd wear
anything right now; even my PE kit.'

She stared at the phone. Shook it. 'Now
what's wrong? I know I charged this thing, but
I can't get it to work. I hope the mud and rain
didn't ruin it.' She shoved the phone back
in the bag. 'I guess that's it then. We can't

perform. We aren't going to be *Tomorrow's Stars* after all.' A tear trickled down her face, cutting a snail trail through a streak of mud on her left cheek.

'Of course we're going to perform,' Elly said. 'I'm not letting a little mud stop me. Come on, let's get going.'

'We can't go looking like this!' Sierra wailed. 'You may not be able to see yourself, Elly, but I can tell you you don't look like a pop princess right now—more like a walking mud pie!'

'Sierra's right,' Tash said, looking from her own mud-splattered skirt and leggings to Sierra and Elly. 'I just don't see how we can go on like this.'

Elly stared at them. 'I've just had a totally crazy but brilliant idea,' she shouted over the music.

'Did she say she's gone crazy?' Sierra asked Tash.

'No!' Elly grabbed their hands. 'Listen! What if we make the mud part of the act?'

'How?' Tash shook her head.

'Poor thing.' Sierra patted Elly on the head. 'It's all too much for you, I know.'

'Like this!' Elly grabbed a fresh handful of mud and smeared it over the front of Tash's purple jacket.

'Hey, stop!' Tash jerked away, but Elly grabbed her.

'Hold still and witness the magic,' she ordered. She carved a peace symbol into the plastered mud. Then she drew stars either side of it. Next she drew a peace symbol on Tash's right cheek and a star on her left.

'Finger paints!' cried Sierra. 'Why not? Let me have a go.' And she advanced on Elly with a fistful of mud. Five minutes later all three of them were decorated head to foot with muddy peace symbols, shooting stars, and spirals. Next, Sierra plastered mud into their hair and twisted it into spikes and twirls.

'We look awesome,' Sierra said.

'Wild and wonderful,' agreed Tash.

'And we're late!' yelped Elly, checking her watch. She grabbed Tash and Sierra by the hands and ran for it.

Chapter 11

The tent flying the banner *Tomorrow's Stars* had people queuing to get inside. Elly's heart skipped a beat as she saw them and she heard Tash's groan of dismay. Music, loud, fast and furious—scarily good music—soared out of the tent to mingle with a dozen other songs dogfighting to control the sound waves of the Sunday Island Music Festival.

It was good that they were a bit late: no time to hesitate or worry. Elly led the way at a run as they rounded the tent to find the artists' entrance. A man and a woman with clipboards and earpieces checked their passes and ID three times, staring disbelievingly at their muddy appearance, before ticking them off the list of finalists and leading them inside, through a litter of cables and machinery, to the side of the tent.

'Hey, girls, keep it clean!' the clipboard man said with a cheeky grin. 'It's a family show.' He howled with laughter at his joke. Sierra rolled her eyes.

Another act was taking the stage. 'You're up next!' shouted the woman. 'Those are the steps up; wait till you're announced over the tannoy.' The man gave them the thumbs up. Then they both rushed away again.

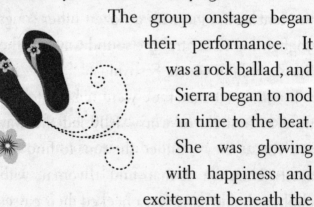

The group onstage began their performance. It was a rock ballad, and Sierra began to nod in time to the beat. She was glowing with happiness and excitement beneath the

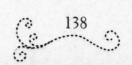

mud. Elly felt the
thud of the bass
in her bones, from
her feet to the top
of her head. The crowd
was clapping and swaying to the music, wolf
whistles split the air and strobe lights played
overhead. It's really happening, Elly told
herself. She gave herself a hug. Her heart was
pounding with excitement.

Someone clutched her hand, and Elly
turned startled eyes to Tash. Beneath the
muddy peace symbol, her friend's face was
as grey as the sides of the tent. Tash shook
her head, eyes miserable. It was too loud to
talk, so Elly did the only thing she could: she
squeezed Tash's hand and mouthed: 'It's OK!'

But it wasn't OK. Tash was in trouble. Elly
smiled reassuringly at her friend, but she was
really worried. Was their dream about to end
in disaster? Her eyes scanned the audience
and she suddenly spotted Marina in front of

the crowd. Elly felt a surge of relief, despite her worry about Tash. If Marina was here maybe the row between the members of The Sparks had been sorted out. Their new friend was in full pop star costume tonight: sparkly jacket, heels, make-up. She was surrounded by officials in suits, minders in hoodies, and adoring fans, but Dorothy stood beside her, looking sane and normal and totally out of place.

The rock ballad ended with a finale equally loud and mournful, and drums and bass crashed to an end. The crowd stamped, clapped and hollered their approval. The competition was tough.

The grip on Elly's hand tightened. She turned to see Tash grab Sierra's arm too. Tash stared at them both. 'I can't do it!' she shouted as the noise of applause began to die down. 'I'm sorry, I just can't go up there. Not in front of Marina!' Tash pointed to the crowd. 'Not looking like this!'

'We can't pull out now!' Sierra looked horrified. 'Come on, Tash. You can do it!'

'I can't! I won't be able to sing a word in front of all these people. I'll die. I really will. And I can't sing Marina's song in front of her covered in mud. Let's go. Please!'

Elly stared at Sierra and shrugged. What could they do? Tash was more important than a contest, even *Tomorrow's Stars*. They would have to cancel their performance. Sierra's brown eyes were filling with tears, but she slowly nodded her head. Tash had to come first.

The tannoy squealed and boomed into life and a strange echo-y voice rang out: 'The next act is local talent. Three Sunday Island girls!

Give a big, warm welcome to The Charms!'

Tash froze, looking trapped and terrified, as applause filled the tent. It swelled, then died slowly away. Silence grew. A few shouts of 'Come on!' from the audience. Elly saw Marina frown with concern, glance over to where they were standing, half hidden by the stage. She caught Elly's eyes. Would she still want to be friends with them after this? Elly bowed her head and turned to leave. Then she heard the last noise she expected in the world:

'Yap! Yap-yap-yap!'

Mojo?

Elly whirled round to search for the dog. She spotted a commotion at the tent entrance and there suddenly was Aunt Dina, looking very tall and very glam in a sparkly sweater and skinny jeans.

She was holding a wriggling, yapping Mojo!

'What?' Tash cried. 'How did he get into the festival?'

'He must have found his way through the gap in the fence we used the other day,' Elly said.

Mojo writhed free of Aunt Dina and jumped to the ground. Security guards lunged, but Mojo dodged them all. He darted through the audience, followed by laughter and cat calls, and headed straight for the stage. He ran right up the steps at the front and then stopped on the stage and began to bark.

'The Charms!' someone bellowed in the audience. 'But there's supposed to be three of them!' Laughter. Mojo barked even louder, and Tash suddenly darted up the steps and on stage. Mojo wagged his tail in delight and ran to greet his mistress, but Tash froze as she faced the audience. She stood, statue-still.

'Come on!' Elly shouted to Sierra, then scrambled up the steps after Tash. Whatever happened, the three of them would see it through together. Elly ran to stand beside Tash. Sierra joined them. Mojo scampered around them once, then ran to the front of the stage and sat down, facing the audience.

'He wants us to perform!' Elly said. 'Look, Tash!'

'It's true!' Sierra gasped. 'The little show-off.'

Tash slowly nodded. 'Let's do it then.'

Elly took a deep breath and looked out over the audience. It was going to happen: they were going to perform after all!

Sierra turned and waved at the technicians backstage. The tannoy crackled again. 'Once more, ladies and gentlemen. We give you The Charms. And

their charming
canine guest!'

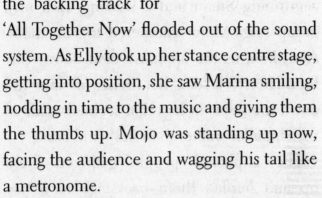

And it began:
the backing track for
'All Together Now' flooded out of the sound
system. As Elly took up her stance centre stage,
getting into position, she saw Marina smiling,
nodding in time to the music and giving them
the thumbs up. Mojo was standing up now,
facing the audience and wagging his tail like
a metronome.

And then it was just the music and the
singing and the dance steps. It lasted for ever
but was over in the blink of an eye. Elly felt
as if she must be shining with sheer happiness
as she sang. She could dance for ever! Tash's
voice soared, sweet and accurate. Sierra
shimmied beside them, her every movement
magical. The last chords rolled away, and
applause took their place. The audience
loved them!

Elly found she was shaking with adrenaline

and happiness. Applause rolled on and on and it felt glorious. This was why she loved performing! She whirled round and gathered a grinning Sierra and a shaking Tash in a group hug. Mojo scampered to join them. And then, as the applause died down, Elly found herself leading her friends off stage and down the steps on legs that seemed made of marshmallow rather than flesh and bone.

The clipboard people gathered them up and herded them backstage to a tiny area crammed with the other finalists. Elly collapsed on a chair and watched Sierra and Tash do the same. Tash was holding Mojo, who sat quietly on her lap as though he was the best-behaved dog in the world.

The last act was performing now. Elly couldn't bring herself to listen properly. She felt

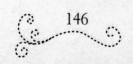

wiped out. It was
too noisy to talk
so she just sat and
waited, like all the
other contestants.

The act ended, and then the applause. This
was it: the judges were deciding now.

Elly caught Tash's and Sierra's eyes and the
three of them stood up and held hands as the
tannoy cut in again. 'Ladies and gentlemen:
the winner of *Tomorrow's Stars* will now be
announced by Marina of The Sparks!'

The staff with clipboards led them back to
the stage. All the acts climbed up to face the
audience, one after the other. Applause rang
through the tent, then faded. Spotlights shone
on Marina, moving through the audience
towards the stage.

'It's gonna be us, it's gonna be us . . .' Sierra
chanted softly.

Elly held her breath as Marina, in her
glittering green and gold jacket, climbed the

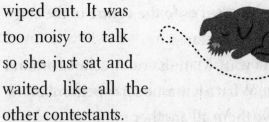

steps and walked onto the centre of the stage to rapturous applause.

'Thank you!' Marina's voice echoed around the tent. 'What a fantastic set of performances. Let's give them all another round of applause to say thanks for such a great evening.' She turned round and clapped herself as the audience went wild. When Elly caught her eye, Marina winked and smiled broadly. Oh wow! Elly's stomach lurched. Could Marina be signalling that they had won?

When the applause faded, Marina turned round to face the audience again. 'There are no winners and losers here. All the acts performing tonight really are *Tomorrow's Stars* and every one of them should be very proud of what they've done tonight. But the judges had a job to do. They had to pick one and it was a tough decision.

'And so: tonight's winner, the group that will perform on the main stage tomorrow at the Sunday Island Music Festival is . . .'

Elly reached out and found Tash's and Sierra's hands. She closed her eyes and wished.

'The winner of *Tomorrow's Stars* is . . . The Frantic Fridays!'

The four skinny teenage boys lounging next to them, dressed in torn jeans, ripped T-shirts and wearing identical I-am-too-cool-to-care expressions, exploded into screams and hugs, bouncing up and down like motorized pogo sticks.

Applause rolled through the tent like an avalanche. Elly opened her eyes and saw the disappointed faces of Sierra and Tash looking back at her. They hadn't won. After all that: after Marina and the mud and Tash and Mojo coming to the rescue. They had still lost.

Sierra shrugged, and began to clap. Tash was clapping too, as well as she could with Mojo bundled in her arms. Elly sighed. They'd done their best. They had given a great performance. She joined in the applause, trying her best to ignore her disappointment.

As the applause dwindled, Marina's amplified voice cut in again. 'Yes, well done to the Frantics. As winners of *Tomorrow's Stars*, they will be performing tomorrow on the main stage!'

Marina grinned at the Frantics as she waited for the fresh applause to die down. Then she turned back to the audience. 'I'm sure we're all looking forward to seeing them perform again. But I have one more announcement. I want to give an honorary mention to my friends, Elly, Tash, and Sierra of

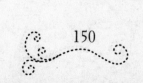

The Charms! Let's hear it for them.'

Elly blinked in surprise and delight as applause began again, and she saw Marina grinning at them over her shoulder.

'The Charms' cover of The Sparks song, 'All Together Now', was simply brilliant. It's a song about friendship, and The Charms sang it beautifully tonight because they meant every word.' Marina paused, her voice suddenly sounding a bit wobbly. 'So, as a special thank you to The Charms for such a brilliant cover, they will be performing with The Sparks tomorrow during our headline slot!'

Marina waved in their direction. Applause burst out again. Sierra screamed at the top of her lungs. Tash looked delighted and horrified at the same time and Mojo began to bark. Elly found she was crying with joy. Sierra bounced from her to Tash, hugging them in turn and shrieking while she did it. Elly hugged her back, hugged Tash, and got a lick on the nose from Mojo.

Finally the applause died down, the audience began streaming out of the tent, and the other finalists climbed off the stage. Elly saw Aunt Dina, Tash's mum and Sierra's dad in a huddle waiting for them. Her aunt caught her eye and waved. There would be celebrations tonight!

As they filed off stage after the other finalists, Marina stepped forward and gave them each a hug. 'You made me cry, you guys. That was so lovely.' She smiled and sniffed at the same time, and Elly saw tears in her eyes. 'Promise me, you three. Promise that you'll never let anything get in the way of your friendship.'

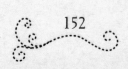

The sadness had come

back to Marina's face, and Elly reached out and gave her a quick hug. 'I promise,' she said, and touched her pendant's silver friendship charm.

'Me too,' Tash said, looking down at her pin.

'Me three!' Sierra held forward her arm with the charm bracelet.

'Excellent! See you tomorrow then.' Marina smiled. 'Um, will the mud theme continue? Should I order a costume change for The Sparks?'

'No!' Sierra said firmly. 'Mud is so last year.'

Elly watched Marina clatter off the stage to join the important-looking people waiting for her. It had been a brilliant evening, but she couldn't help wondering why Marina was the only one of The Sparks to show up tonight. Suddenly, she knew she had to find out. Marina had given the three of them a special gift tonight, the gift of a lifetime. Elly couldn't watch her new friend's unhappiness and not try to help.

Chapter 12

Elly had dreamt about the concert all night, dreamt about Mojo barking as he ran onstage. She could still hear him barking, even though now she was half awake. She opened a bleary eye. It was morning. Sunlight slanted through her attic window. And Mojo was still barking!

Not a dream then. A Mojo-gram from the Tash messaging service. And that usually meant trouble! Despite the late night, Elly was suddenly wide awake. She pulled on shorts, a T-shirt and her flip-flops and slid down the ladder from her loft bedroom, landing with a soft thump. Best not to wake Aunt Dina if

Mojo hadn't already done so. It felt early.

She padded downstairs and slipped the latch on the front door. Mojo had stopped barking as soon as he heard her at the door. Now he stood on the doorstep, whining with impatience.

'I know, I know,' Elly soothed. She found the message tube velcroed to his collar and slid the note out. *'Emergency meeting at tree house. ASAP!'*

Elly took a moment to write Aunt Dina a note, then grabbed her fleece from the hook beside the door and followed Mojo outside and up the hill towards Sunday House. It was early enough to be chilly, and Elly was glad of a run to warm up.

She wound her way through the maze which hid the tree house at its heart, and in less than ten

minutes was climbing
the rope ladder up to
the wooden platform
and front door, which
was standing wide open. Mojo greeted her.
Somehow he had got there ahead of her. Elly
cuddled him under her arm and climbed to
the platform.

'Sierra's not here yet.' Tash was pacing back
and forth in the middle of the tree house's
single room. 'But am I glad to see you! I've
got some bad news.'

'Bad news?' Sierra's head appeared at the
top of the ladder and Elly gave her a hand
up. 'Of course it's bad news. That dog never
brings good news. So what's up?' She was
yawning and still in PJs with a fleece over
the top. 'I'm hungry and short of sleep, so it'd
better be important!'

'It is.' Tash closed the tree house door and
slumped down on a floor cushion. Elly and
Sierra sat beside her. Mojo crawled on Tash's

lap and proceeded to go to sleep, his job done. 'Here goes,' said Tash. 'The Sparks are breaking up.'

Elly felt her stomach lurch. 'What? Are you sure?'

'How do you know?' Sierra asked. 'This is probably just some rumour . . . '

'No rumour,' Tash interrupted. 'It hasn't been announced officially yet, but I overheard Mum on the phone last night to the other festival committee members. Emergency phone call. The Sparks have pulled out of the festival!'

The news hit Elly like a thump in the chest. She couldn't believe it. 'Why? I mean, what were they arguing about really? What could be this important—to make them break up?' She felt like crying.

'No!' Sierra cried. 'They

can't! What about our performance with them?'

'What about the festival?' Tash said, shaking her head. 'People might demand their money back.'

'What about Marina, Abi, and Lou's friendship?' Elly said. Poor Marina. This must be why she'd looked so sad last night when she was talking about how important it was to stay friends.

'I can't believe this is happening!' Sierra jumped to her feet and began to prowl around the tree house. 'Our one chance to appear onstage with The Sparks . . . and they break up! I mean, how typical—'

She broke off as the chorus of 'All Together Now' rang out. 'What is that?'

The chorus repeated again. 'Great ring tone, Sierra. How did you get that?' Elly said when she realized the sound was coming from Sierra's handbag.

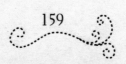

Sierra rootled around in her handbag and answered the phone just as the ringing stopped. 'That's strange,' she said, turning the phone over and over in her hands. The phone pinged with a message.

'Who's calling you at this time of the morning?' Tash asked.

'At least your phone's working now,' Elly said.

'It was out of charge,' Sierra said. 'Which is totally weird because I remember charging it. But hey, everyone's losing their minds at the moment.' She sighed. 'This'll be Dad with more bad news I bet . . .' Sierra's voice trailed away as she put the phone to her ear to listen to the voicemail message. Her frown of disappointment faded as she listened. Elly watched with surprise as Sierra's mouth fell open in shock. What now? Was it really even more bad news?

'What's the matter?' Tash demanded.

Sierra hung up and stared at the phone in shock. 'This . . . this isn't my phone! It's Marina's. You remember we were comparing at lunch at her gran's yesterday. And Marina had to leave in a rush? She must have picked my phone by mistake, 'cause this is definitely hers.'

'Well . . . that's not the end of the world. You can just give it back to her gran to give to her,' Elly said. 'Why do you look so freaked out?'

'You don't understand,' Sierra stuttered.

'Then explain!' Tash reached out and tugged on her pyjama leg. 'Come on, spill.'

'I know why The Sparks broke up,' Sierra announced.

'You've lost it,' Tash said, shaking her head.

'No! Really.' Sierra bit her lip and stared down at the phone. 'Look, you guys. I know you should never listen to someone else's

messages, but obviously I didn't mean to . . .
and now I know something. I can't stop
knowing it, can I? I think you need to hear
this too.'

'We shouldn't—' Elly began.

Sierra pressed a button on the phone,
switching to speakerphone, and a woman's
voice filled the tree house.

'Marina, darling, it's Lisa. I've just heard
from FastPlay again. Listen, the record
company has come back and they've doubled
their original offer if you'll sign. Doubled,
Marina! Can you do the maths? Because I
can. OK, I know you don't want
to leave The Sparks, but a
solo career is the way
to go. This is your
chance for a huge
career and these
chances don't come
along every day. You
know that as well as I do.

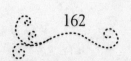

I need you to think about this offer seriously, Marina. You've turned them down three times now, and they won't keep coming back. I'm telling you, as your manager, you can't afford to turn a solo deal like this down. Get back to me. *Ciao*.'

Tash jumped to her feet and took the phone from Sierra. She switched it off. 'It's wrong to listen to other people's voice messages,' she said.

'But this is why the band's been arguing,' Sierra cried. 'Abi and Lou must have heard rumours about this deal. They think Marina's going to break up The Sparks and go solo. But this proves she doesn't want to do that.'

'Maybe, but there's nothing we can do about it,' Tash said. 'We need to give this back to Marina as soon as we can.'

'There has to be *something* we can do,'

Elly interrupted. 'It's no good saying it's not our business, Tash. And I know we shouldn't have heard that message, but we did. Now we know about it we have to try to sort things out. Don't you remember how you felt when our friendship was nearly wrecked because your mum believed something about her friends that wasn't true?'

Tash bit her lip and her cheeks turned pink. Their mothers had been best friends on Sunday Island when they were girls, but a treasure belonging to Tash's mum had gone missing and she had blamed her two best friends for it. The silver charms Elly, Tash, and Sierra wore were the only reminders of that long-ago friendship.

'OK,' Tash said. 'If you can think of some way we can clear things up between The Sparks,

I'm willing to help.'

Elly frowned, thinking.

'Couldn't we just tell Abi and Lou about the message?' Sierra asked.

'They don't even know us,' Tash replied. 'Why should they believe a word we say?'

'I've got it!' Elly cried. 'I've just had a brilliant idea.' The others turned to look at her. Elly took a deep breath. 'Here's the plan . . .'

Chapter 13

'I'm not sure we'll pull it off,' Sierra muttered for the tenth time. 'Why should they believe us?'

'We've got to try something even if it means telling a little white lie.' Tash tweaked Sierra's hair, pulling it over her face. 'Cheer up, grumpy!'

Sierra's bottom lip drooped. 'But if it goes wrong we'll get in so much trouble.'

'They'll probably put us in prison,' Tash said, her round blue eyes solemn. 'You don't look your best in striped pyjamas, Sierra. And I don't think lifers get let out for shopping

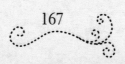

trips.' She broke down into splutters of laughter. Mojo opened a sleepy eye.

'Very funny.' Sierra huffed and rolled her eyes.

'It's the only plan I can think of,' Elly said with a sigh. 'You don't have to join in, Sierra, if you don't want to. But I have to do something to help Marina. She's our friend.'

Sierra looked from Elly to Tash. She shrugged. 'OK. You're right. We gotta try.'

'Great! You should probably get going,' Elly said. 'And take Mojo. He can charm anyone into doing anything!' She pushed Sierra and Tash towards the tree house door.

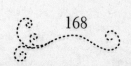

They lowered a yawning Mojo down in his lift basket, then Elly followed the others down the rope ladder. She waved them off. 'Good luck! See you in an hour!'

This has got to work, Elly muttered to herself as she followed her friends through the maze. As soon as they were clear, Tash and Sierra loped off. Elly watched them out of sight, then began to run towards the far end of town and Dorothy's cottage.

Elly finally puffed up the lane to the front door and rang the bell. Dorothy opened the door at once. She looked different—suddenly old and frail. She nodded when she saw Elly. 'Good,' she said. 'Just what she needs, I think. Try to cheer her up, my dear. I don't seem to be able to do much good.'

Dorothy opened the sitting room door and closed it once Elly had stepped inside. Elly heard her footsteps trailing towards the back of the house.

'She'll be off to work in her garden now,'

Marina said. She was sitting on the sofa, wrapped in a cardigan despite the August sunshine and cradling a cup of tea in her hands. 'It's how she sorts things out when she's upset. Sometimes I think I ought to take up gardening.' She smiled wanly at Elly. 'Hi there. Congratulations again for last night. I'll never forget your performance: it meant a lot. But I'm afraid I've got bad news to tell you . . .' her voice faded.

Elly walked over to sit beside her on the sofa. Marina's eyes were red and swollen— she'd obviously been crying. 'Don't worry,' Elly said. 'I've heard the news. I'm really sorry.'

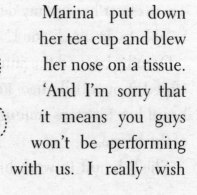

Marina put down her tea cup and blew her nose on a tissue. 'And I'm sorry that it means you guys won't be performing with us. I really wish

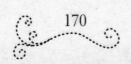

I could change
things but . . .'
She sighed and put
her head in her hands.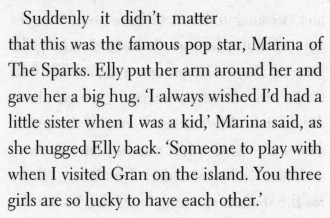

Suddenly it didn't matter
that this was the famous pop star, Marina of
The Sparks. Elly put her arm around her and
gave her a big hug. 'I always wished I'd had a
little sister when I was a kid,' Marina said, as
she hugged Elly back. 'Someone to play with
when I visited Gran on the island. You three
girls are so lucky to have each other.'

'I know,' Elly said. 'But friends happen when
you least expect it. I mean, I never expected
to meet you.' She paused. She had to do this
just right. Her plan to get The Sparks back
together had to work. It just had to. 'You need
something to get your mind off all this yucky
stuff. You need my Aunt Dina's special fudge
brownies. They are so good. She was making
a batch when I left. You'll like Aunt Dina.
She's such a big fan, and she's totally cool. I

bet you'd make friends too.'

Marina smiled at her. 'Gran's told me lots about Dina. She sounds really nice. And the brownies sound great too!' She sprang to her feet, looking relieved to have something to do. 'All right, let's go. It can't do any good moping here. I'll just get a jacket and tell Gran I'm off. She's worried enough about me as it is.' Marina strode out of the room, then came back a few minutes later wearing a denim jacket and dark sunglasses. 'Sorry for the shades,' she said, 'but I don't want the world seeing I've been crying. Everything gets in the tabloids, whether it's true or not.'

Elly led her out of town and up the path towards Sunday House. They walked along, chatting for a while. Then Marina seemed to notice where they were heading.

'Why are we going towards Sunday House?' Her voice was puzzled. 'Doesn't your aunt live near town?'

'I thought I could quickly show you the tree house first,' Elly said, crossing her fingers behind her back. It felt wrong to lie to Marina, even a little. But if it got The Sparks back together . . . She cleared her throat with a little cough. 'I remembered you said you wanted to see it. And the brownies won't be ready yet.'

'OK,' Marina said. 'Great—the tree house sounds really cool.'

Elly glanced sideways at Marina. The pop star looked too deep in her own thoughts to pay much attention to anything else. Eyes hidden behind dark sunglasses, shoulders hunched under her denim jacket, Marina strode up the hill beside Elly without saying another word.

Until they got to the maze. 'The tree house

is in there? Are you serious? I got so lost in that maze once when I was a kid. I knew I was trespassing and I got scared Old Man Blake would find me and have me locked up!'

'Don't worry,' Elly said. 'I know the way through. Just follow me.'

They wound along the twisting paths of the maze between tall walls of dark green yew. 'Wow, this is so creepy!' Marina said. She sounded nervous. 'No way would I do this on my own. Are we getting close yet?'

'You sound just like Sierra!' Elly said with a giggle.

Marina laughed.

And then the path kinked right and they were out into the clearing. The giant tree in the middle of the maze reared overhead, spreading its mossy grey arms wide. Marina gazed up and

her eyes widened
as she saw the tree
house nestled in the
crook of two enormous
branches.

'Oh my . . . ' she breathed. 'That was worth
the walk, Elly. So that's the famous tree house?'

'Yes,' Elly said, feeling very proud. 'It
belongs to Tash, of course, but the three of us
sleep over here and have midnight feasts and
stuff. It's sort of our meeting house.'

'That's so cool. Can I go up?' In a moment,
Marina was scampering up the ladder. She
turned at the top and grinned over her
shoulder at Elly. 'I hope you've organized a
midnight feast even if it is daytime. Starring
your aunt's fudge brownies!'

'Now you really *do* sound like Sierra.' Elly
stepped onto the bottom rung of the ladder
and began to pull herself up. 'Just be patient.
All will be revealed.' She tried to keep her
voice cheery, but her mouth had gone

cottony-dry with nerves. There was so much
that could go wrong . . .

Marina scrambled onto the platform and
turned to give Elly a hand up. Then she
took off her sunglasses and shoved them in
her jacket pocket. 'Shall I?' She nodded at
the door.

'I think you should go in first,' Elly said.
Heart thumping, she pushed open the tree
house door and stood back to let Marina enter.

Marina strode inside then jerked to a stop
when she saw who was waiting. Tash and
Sierra stood in the middle of the room, and
beside them, looking harassed and puzzled,
were Abi and Lou. The Sparks
were reunited.

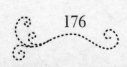
Lou spotted Marina
and frowned. Abi,
who was only Tash-
sized, drew herself
up as tall as she could
as her smile faded.

'What are you doing here?' Marina asked in a chilly voice. She turned to Elly, a hurt look in her eyes. 'Why have you done this?'

'I can explain!' Elly was feeling flustered now. Was it all going to blow up in their faces? Had she just made things worse?

'Well, I hope someone can,' Abi said. 'Because these kids told us you'd asked to meet here to apologize for breaking up The Sparks.' She turned an accusing glare on Tash, then Sierra. 'They knew all about your gran and her house, so I thought they were for real and you'd sent them. That's the only reason I came. Because we used to be friends. But it's pretty clear you weren't expecting us.'

'We've been tricked,' Lou said, staring from Tash and Sierra to Elly and back. 'It was the dog who got to me.' She glanced at Mojo, who wagged his tail when he saw her looking at him. 'I always was a sucker for cute dogs.

But now I want to know what's going on here.'

'I'm sorry.' Elly stepped forward into the middle of the room between the warring Sparks. 'I lied to Marina to get her here. And I had Tash and Sierra lie to you. It's just that we think you need to talk to each other. This is all a mistake. The Sparks can't just break up.'

'Now I've heard everything!' Lou exploded.

'You girls are trying to be kind . . . probably,' Abi added, her eyes doubtful. 'But you don't know what's been going on. There's no point us staying here. I'm off.'

'Yeah,' Lou said. 'Me too.'

Elly stared at them in dismay. It couldn't end this way. But what could she do to stop it?

Chapter 14

'Fine,' said Marina. 'You two run away, but before you go I want to clear the air. I can't *believe* you're looking for a new lead singer.'

Abi and Lou glanced at each other with puzzled looks.

'What are you talking about?' Lou shook her head. 'Don't try to blame us. What about you? You're the dark horse. Keeping secrets from your best friends? I thought friends were supposed to talk about everything. Trust each other. Well, we've heard the rumours. We've read the tabloids. We know about the solo recording deal, so just stop pretending, Marina.'

'The tabloids have got it wrong, again. You can't tell me you take that rubbish seriously?' Marina cried. 'I don't want to leave the band!'

'Tell that to Lisa,' Abi said. 'She's had a word with us, Marina. We know. We know what she's worked out for you.'

'You don't know anything. Have you asked me? No, you just go off in a huff and try to get another lead singer.'

'Lead singer? What lead singer?' Lou threw her hands up in the air. 'I've had enough of this.'

'You're not listening to each other!' Elly cried.

But it was too late. Lou headed for the door, followed by a tight-lipped Abi. Marina turned her back and stared out of the window.

Elly could have screamed

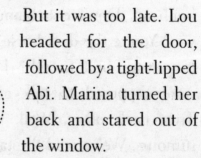

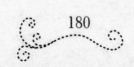

in frustration. Instead she darted in front of the doorway. Sierra and Tash came running and Elly locked arms with them, standing squarely in front of the only way out.

'No, girls. This isn't going to work,' Abi said gently. 'Out of the way, please.'

'You can leave in a minute,' Elly said. 'But first you need to hear something.'

She nodded to Sierra, who pulled out Marina's pink phone, and punched some buttons. 'Um, sorry about this, Marina, but I think it will sort everything out.' The speaker phone came on at once and repeated the message Sierra had discovered earlier. Marina jerked around in surprise as the sound of their manager's voice filled the tree house.

The recorded voice ended and silence filled the room.

Three shocked and silent Sparks stared at each other.

Elly cleared her throat. 'Sierra and Marina have the same phone. They got them mixed up a few days ago and Sierra heard this message by mistake. We're sorry for listening to your private voicemail, Marina. We didn't mean to. It's only that after we heard this, and then we heard you guys were breaking up . . . we had to do something!'

Marina turned to them. She looked dazed. 'It's OK,' she said gently. 'You meant well, I know.' She fished in her jeans pocket, pulled out a pink phone and handed it to Sierra.

'You'd better have yours back. I had no idea it wasn't mine. I turned it off, you see. I didn't want Lisa nagging me any more about the record deal.'

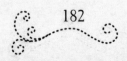

Abi and Lou were

staring at Marina as though her hair had turned bright green.

'I'm so sorry,' Abi said at last. 'I should have known you'd never run out on us.'

'You know,' Lou said gruffly, her face turning pink, 'you *are* talented enough for that solo career. You should think it over, like Lisa says.'

'So you can have your new lead singer, right?' Marina shook her head. 'So who is it? Who are you dumping me for?'

'We're not!' Abi shouted. 'If Lisa told you we wanted someone else, then she's lied about that too. I can't believe her.'

'The Sparks are me, you, and Abi, Marina,' Lou said, her voice quiet and gentle. 'No one else. We just thought you wanted out. Lisa may be a total liar, but she's right: you'd go places faster on your own.'

'Would *you* do that?' Marina frowned at

her friends in disbelief. 'Would you ditch *me* for fame and money? Is that what our band is about? What our friendship is about? Because I always thought it was more than that.'

Lou sniffed, her eyes wet with tears. 'Oh, Marina, I'm so sorry!'

'I'm sorry too,' Marina said. She bit her lip. 'Lisa told me you were looking for a new lead singer and I believed her! I should have known she was lying. I think it's time we got a new manager.'

'So are we back?' Abi asked, her face pale.

'What about it, Marina?' Lou's voice was whisper-quiet. Elly could hardly hear her.

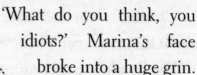

'What do you think, you idiots?' Marina's face broke into a huge grin. The next moment The Sparks were hugging, crying and talking all at once.

'They sound just like us,'

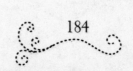

Sierra said. 'Aren't they supposed to be grown-ups?'

Elly just laughed. She didn't want to talk. She just wanted to watch three best friends making up.

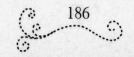

Chapter 15

Elly knew she would never forget the final night of the Sunday Island Music Festival. Or the look on her dad's face when he arrived at Aunt Dina's cottage.

'Elly!' He pulled her into his arms for a bear hug. Her eyes welled with tears. She had missed him so much. 'Let me look at you,' he said and held her away from him.

'How do you like my costume?' Elly said, spinning around. Sierra had come over earlier to give Elly a super-star make-over before her dad showed up.

She saw tears in her dad's bright blue eyes.

'You look so grown up,' he said with a sniff. 'I've been hearing a little bit about what you get up to when my back is turned.'

Aunt Dina stopped arranging her hand-crocheted evening wrap around her shoulders and winked at Elly.

'I'm really proud of you, Elly,' Dad said. 'Not just for being a real trouper, like your mum, but for being a good friend. Now come on, I can't wait to see this famous performance.'

They arrived at the main stage in between bands. The Sparks' roadies scurried around the stage, setting up. Aunt Dina and the other grown-ups handed them over to the festival officials and Elly found herself hustled to the side of the stage. She spotted Marina and the other Sparks waiting just ahead of her. Then the tannoy cut over the crowd noise, announcing:

188

'The Sparks!'

Across the field, clapping, whistles, and cheers rose up. Elly watched Marina, Lou, and Abi leap onto the stage. The applause grew louder. And then it was their turn! Even Tash didn't have time to be nervous as they were bustled up the stairs and onto the stage. Marina, looking glamorous in a long shimmering green tunic and knee high boots, just like Elly's, grabbed a microphone. The applause faded slowly, and the field grew silent.

'We nearly didn't make it tonight,' Marina's voice boomed over the sound system. 'And so our first song is dedicated to some very good friends of ours, who made it happen. Three girls who are best friends as well as great performers. Let's hear it for The Charms and 'All Together Now'!'

Lou hit the drums, nodding at Marina

and Abi as she rapped out a heavy beat. Abi bopped in time to the beat, and the keyboard joined in. They both grinned at Marina, who broke into a glorious smile as she lifted up her guitar and struck the first chord. The Sparks were back together!

Elly danced and sang as she never had before. Tash and Sierra joined in either side of her, singing their hearts out. It was good. It was beyond good. It was like flying!

All too soon, the music ended. Then applause began. And more applause. Elly found herself pushed and tugged to the front of the stage. The Sparks stood to one side and clapped with the audience. Elly held Tash and Sierra by the hand and they stood in a row to take their bows. Not one, not two, but three bows, as an enthusiastic audience screamed, clapped and whistled their appreciation. At the back of the field, audience members seated on picnic rugs shifted and shuffled to their feet. It was a standing ovation!

Aunt Dina smiled up at Elly a few rows from the front of the stage. And beside her stood Dad. His eyes caught Elly's as she rose from the last bow, and she saw love shining there as sparkly and bright as the silver friendship charm her mother had left behind. Mum had known all about love. She would have been so proud right now. Elly put her arms around her friends and hugged them tight.

It was a perfect moment. A perfect moment in a perfect flip-flop summer.

A Note from the Author

I grew up in Missouri, as far from the sea as it is possible to be in the United States. The long, hot summer holidays were spent swimming and canoeing on the lakes and rivers. My sisters, cousins and I watched crayfish wriggle along the creekbeds, waded in the streams and had our toes nibbled by swarms of minnows darting through the clear limestone waters. We snorkelled in the lakes and pretended we were diving among coral reefs and rainbow-coloured fish instead of Missouri mud and whiskery catfish. Childhood summers were full of barbecues, homemade ice cream, watermelon and twilight evenings spent catching fireflies in order to let them go and watch them spiral into the air like sparks from a bonfire.

All the time I was growing up, I longed to see the ocean and finally did on a school trip when I was the same age as Elly, Tash and Sierra. I'll never forget swimming with my friends in the sea for the first time.

Now I live in England with my family, and every summer, we spend as much time as we can on an island. My love for British islands is a big part of the joy of writing the Flip-Flop books. On my first trip to the Isles of Scilly I fell in love with the small whiskery dog of one of the boatmen: a proper seadog who trotted around the boat taking us between the islands with a cocky assurance that charmed me. I've been waiting ever since for a chance to write about Mojo! As I write, I'm taken back to some of my favourite places on earth, places very much like Sunday Island.

Ellen Richardson x

Activities
and
Quizzes

Character Profiles

Elly

Full name: Eleanor Porter
Likes: Adventures, sleepovers, films, acting, and hugs
Dislikes: Friends falling out
Favourite colour: Green
Most treasured possession: The necklace that used to belong to my mum
Star struck dream: To be an actress

Sierra

Full name: Sierra Cruz
Likes: Dancing, fashion, and food! Especially sparkly flip-flops and Aunt Dina's cookies!
Dislikes: Anything scary—including scary noises, scary outfits, and the dark
Favourite colour: Hot hot hot pink
Most treasured possession: My friends. And my huge purple handbag, of course!
Star struck dream: To dance on the stage

Tash

Full name: Natasha Blake-Reynolds
Likes: Surfing, sailing, being outdoors, and animals
Dislikes: Letting my friends down, and wearing heels!
Favourite colour: Purple
Most treasured possession: My dog, Mojo
Star struck dream: To sail around the world

Mojo

Full name: Mojo cute-cuddly-and-cool Blake-Reynolds
Likes: Tash, cuddles, treats, digging,
and making new friends
Dislikes: Sitting still
Star struck dream: To have a never-ending
supply of dog biscuits!

You

Full name: --

Likes: ---

Dislikes: ---

Favourite colour: ------------------------------

Most treasured possession: -----------------

Star struck dream: -----------------------------

Pop Star Personality Quiz

Do you shine in the limelight or cower in the shadows? Perhaps you're better behind the scenes, or maybe you just haven't been brave enough to step out in front of the curtain yet! Do this quiz to find out which of the Flip-Flop Club pop stars you're most like.

1. **How would you feel about talking to a large group of people?**
    a. Really confident—I like being the centre of attention!
    b. A bit nervous at first but I'd enjoy it once I got started.
    c. Terrified! I'd hate to have so many eyes on me!

2. **If you were a pop star, what would you sing about?**
    a. Myself! I'm my own inspiration.
    b. Things that make me feel happy.
    c. Things from the natural world, such as animals, oceans, and wild winds!

3. **What's your fashion style?**
   a. Bold and bright! I like to make a statement.
   b. I like beautiful patterns and nice fabrics—but just for special occasions.
   c. Anything practical that I can get a bit mucky without worrying about.

4. **What's your favourite kind of film?**
   a. Chick flicks! Anything really girly and fun.
   b. Musicals are great—but I like anything with a good story.
   c. Action adventures are my favourite!

5. **What's your favourite way to spend a Saturday afternoon?**
   a. Performing the dance routine I've been working on, and teaching my friends the moves.
   b. Eating cakes and chatting to my friends.
   c. Doing something outdoors—sailing, surfing, dog-walking, or just exploring!

6. **What's your favourite colour?**
   a. Hot pink.
   b. Emerald green.
   c. Purple.

7. **How do you react to criticism?**
   a. I ignore it! As long as I'm having fun it doesn't matter what other people think.
   b. I'd just make sure I was doing the best I could—no one can ask for more than that.
   c. It can make me a bit upset, but it's easier to hear if it's coming from my friends.

8. **If you were a rich and famous pop star, where would you live?**
   a. In a huge mansion in Hollywood!
   b. I'd stay close to my friends and family—they'd keep my feet on the ground!
   c. By the sea, somewhere quiet where I could have dogs and see dolphins from my window.

Mostly a's: Like Sierra, you love performing! You're dedicated and determined, and being the centre of attention means you can show everyone just how great you are! Keep working hard to achieve your dreams—the sky's the limit! Just remember that not everyone is as confident as you are—take care not to push other people into the shadows while you take the limelight.

Mostly b's: Like Elly, you're a natural on stage, even if you sometimes get nervous. Remember that stage fright is only natural, and it's a sign that you're pushing yourself—which is a good thing! Don't be afraid to step out of your comfort zone and try new things. Your true friends will be there to support you!

Mostly c's: Like Tash, you don't like being the centre of attention. It can be really scary having lots of people watching you, especially if you don't feel confident about what you're doing. But don't be too hard on yourself—smile and nobody will notice your mistakes! Remember that everyone's good at different things—you included!

Music Mix Up

The girls have got their headphones tangled! Can you figure out who's listening to what?

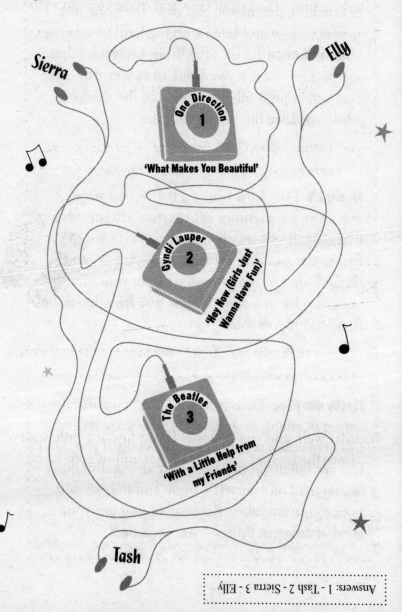

Mud Body Scrub

If you liked the sound of Elly, Tash, and Sierra's mud fight, you'll love this mud body scrub! Rub it on your skin to get rid of any dead cells and make your skin glow!

You will need

- 250g sugar (white, brown, or cane)
- 5 tablespoons coffee granules
- 100ml vegetable oil (almond oil, olive oil, or baby oil will also work)
- 1 teaspoon peppermint extract
- 1 teaspoon vanilla extract

Method

1. Mix sugar and coffee.

2. Add small amounts of oil to the sugar/coffee mix until everything is coated.

3. Add the peppermint and vanilla to fragrance the scrub.

4. Mix well, and you're done! If you find it a little watery from the oil, just add more sugar and/or coffee.

A few tips

★ If you have sensitive skin, do not use coffee granules and use brown sugar (as it's less abrasive).

✦ If you would like a coarser scrub, try using less sugar and more coffee.

Word Search

One of the words on the right *isn't* in this grid. Can you figure out which one's missing?

S	B	D	X	E	M	G	U	I	T	A	R
U	I	E	S	U	O	H	E	E	R	T	D
N	A	E	S	C	J	W	P	Z	H	C	V
G	V	I	R	Q	O	H	K	G	S	I	F
L	C	F	T	R	W	G	I	P	X	R	E
A	Q	J	X	N	A	R	O	J	I	A	S
S	C	I	K	V	F	L	X	E	E	T	T
S	M	A	Z	E	F	G	N	Y	L	S	I
E	R	Y	G	P	W	D	Y	T	L	P	V
S	H	A	I	R	S	P	R	A	Y	O	A
B	T	L	R	E	M	M	U	S	Q	P	L
S	F	N	Z	V	B	W	T	A	S	H	C

ELLY   TASH   SIERRA

MOJO   FRIENDS

FLIP FLOPS   MAZE

POPSTAR   TREEHOUSE

STAGEFRIGHT

MAKEUP

GUITAR

SUNGLASSES

MUSIC   HAIRSPRAY

FESTIVAL

SUMMER

Aunt Dina's Special Spicy Gingerbread Cookies

You will need an adult helper when it comes to using the oven.

Ingredients

- 350g self-raising flour
- 2 teaspoons ground ginger
- ¾ teaspoon ground cinnamon
- ¼ teaspoon ground cloves
- A pinch of salt
- 200g margarine, softened
- 175g light brown soft sugar
- 1 egg
- 1 tablespoon water
- 100ml black treacle
- caster sugar for dusting

Method

1. Preheat oven to 180°C/350°F/Gas Mark 4 and prepare two baking trays with greaseproof baking paper.

2. Sift together the flour, ginger, cinnamon, cloves, and salt. Set aside.

3. In a large bowl, cream together the margarine and sugar until light and fluffy.

4. Beat in the egg, then stir in the water and treacle.

5. Gradually stir the sifted ingredients into the treacle mixture.

6. Place spoonfuls of the dough two inches apart on the prepared baking trays, and flatten slightly. Sprinkle some caster sugar over them.

7. Bake for 8 to 10 minutes in the preheated oven.

8. Allow cookies to cool on baking trays for 5 minutes before removing to a wire rack to cool completely.

Mmmmm . . . chewy, melt-in-your-mouth goodness!

Staragram!

Unscramble the letters in the stars to fill in the blanks below:

F _ _ _ _ _ _ / F _ _ / E _ _ _

This is the password to the top-secret members-only area on The Flip-Flop Club website!

www.the-flip-flop-club.com

**Turn over to read an extract
of the very first book in
The Flip-Flop Club series.**

Elly hated this stupid island. She'd rather be back in London—at least she'd have her friends, even if they did treat her differently now that she was the girl with the dead mum. Her aunt marched on, head erect, eyes forward.

They passed through the hillocks of marram grass lining the beach and emerged onto the main road. Elly had to trot to keep up as Aunt Dina surged up the high street.

'Disappearing for hours on end without a word to tell me where you've gone or when you'll be back. After today I dread to think what other hare-brained things you might get up to. Your best jeans ripped to shreds yesterday. Just how did you do that?'

While trying to keep from being bored to death. Elly remembered her attempt at sandboarding yesterday, using a bit of planking she'd found behind the garden shed, and winced. She opened her mouth to explain.

'No!' said Aunt Dina. 'Don't tell me. I don't want to know!'

She hadn't finished her lecture. Up the hill and

onto the lane, every word blaring, tourists turning to stare. By the time they reached the cottage, Elly was so full of shiny embarrassment she thought she would burst.

How was she going to get through this summer? She had been exiled to Sunday Island as soon as school had finished. Did Dad expect her to spend the whole summer without friends? Or TV? Aunt Dina thought TV rotted your brain. The island didn't even have a cinema. There was only one internet café and that was shut half the time.

She plopped down at her desk and fished her mobile out of the drawer. Dad *had* to let her come home. She punched in his number but nothing happened. No signal again. Sunday-Rubbish-Island had bad mobile reception on top of everything else.

Elly dropped the phone onto the desk, kicked off her trainers and headed for her bed. It was then that she saw it. A bright purple envelope, lying on top of her pillow. And scrawled across it were the words:

SUPER SECRET!
FOR ELLY PORTER'S EYES ONLY.